THE DRYGULCHERS

The ranchers who settled in the Yellow Hills didn't know why Dowie Burke, the meanest gunman they'd ever met, had turned his gang on them. Suddenly the hell-shooting roughs began picking the ranchers off their land like tin cans on a fence, shooting without mercy.

What the settlers never guessed was that their Yellow Hills were filled with a mineral called sulphur, enough to make them rich if they lived to learn the truth. It was Ranger Jim Hatfield's job to see that they did—a job he had to handle alone . . .

Leslie Scott was born in Lewisburg, West Virginia. During the Great War, he joined the French Foreign Legion and spent four years in the trenches. In the 1920s he worked as a mining engineer and bridge builder in the western American states and in China before settling in New York. A bar-room discussion in 1934 with Leo Margulies, who was managing editor for Standard Magazines, prompted Scott to try writing fiction. He went on to create two of the most notable series characters in Western pulp magazines. In 1936, Standard Magazines launched, and in *Texas Rangers*, Scott under the house name of **Jackson Cole** created Jim Hatfield, Texas Ranger, a character whose popularity was so great with readers that this magazine featuring his adventures lasted until 1958. When others eventually began contributing Jim Hatfield stories, Scott created another Texas Ranger hero, Walt Slade, better known as *El Halcon*, the Hawk, whose exploits were regularly featured in *Thrilling Western*. In the 1950s Scott moved quickly into writing book-length adventures about both Jim Hatfield and Walt Slade in long series of original paperback Westerns. At the same time, however, Scott was also doing some of his best work in hardcover Westerns published by Arcadia House; thoughtful, well-constructed stories, with engaging characters and authentic settings and situations. Among the best of these, surely, are *Silver City* (1953), *Longhorn Empire* (1954), *The Trail Builders* (1956), and *Blood on the Rio Grande* (1959). In these hardcover Westerns, many of which have never been reprinted, Scott proved himself highly capable of writing traditional Western stories with characters who have sufficient depth to change in the course of the narrative and with a degree of authenticity and historical accuracy absent from many of his series stories.

THE DRYGULCHERS

Jackson Cole

GUNSMOKE

This hardback edition 2002
by Chivers Press
by arrangement with
Golden West Literary Agency

ISBN 0 7540 8202 4

British Library Cataloguing in Publication Data available.

Printed and bound in Great Britain by
BOOKCRAFT, Midsomer Norton, Somerset

CHAPTER I

Careful Killers

Night had just fallen over the Yellow Hills. A warm wind rustled the dry summer foliage and sudden gusts picked up dust from bare spots, to deposit a coating of fine particles on whatever was handy.

A dozen riders silently approached the small cabin nestling in the meadow between two summits. An oil lamp inside acted as a beacon, shining through a small window in the front wall by the door. "Keep it quiet," warned the burly leader as they drew closer. "The old goat can shoot out a squirrel's eye at a hundred yards."

The rising moon touched his hard face. Its silver glow swept the Texas country along the lower Colorado River, the stream widening and slowing down as it neared the Gulf plains.

Houston lay a day's ride eastward and a hundred miles or so to the northwest stood Austin, now capital of the Lone Star State.

There were still ranchers in the district but they were small operators, for since the Civil War the big outfits had moved or set up far to the west to avoid the crowding as farmers and crop growers came in. The beef market had been developed into a huge industry since the end of the war, and cowmen could afford to be lords of all they surveyed in the tremendous open spaces in west Texas.

An emigrant to the country, Lon Styles, sat in that one-room shack, which he had built from local timber with his own hands when he had settled his homestead.

His long-booted feet were on the slab table and he had just finished his supper of beans and fried pork and coffee, cooked on his old iron stove.

He had lost his wife and children during the terrible war which had raged between brothers for four years. Hunger and privation had weakened his family and when they had fled from their plantation in Kentucky at the approach of enemy raiders, disease had claimed them, as it often did in such times.

Styles had come West with a fellow officer from the Southern armies. His friend had been a colonel of cavalry, and Styles a major. They had been boyhood comrades in the bluegrass region. His old crony, Moss Jordan, now lived not too far away.

Lon Styles was drawn and thin, but he had won in the bitter struggle with fate and had maintained his nerve, and his eyes were alert. His clothing, made up of bits of his old gray uniform and what he had managed to purchase during the years, was clean enough, but patched by a soldier's own hands. His saber hung on a wooden peg driven into the wall and the felt campaign hat with which he covered his sparse hair was on the table.

Styles was reading a month-old newspaper sympathetic to the Lost Cause, a clandestine sheet distributed by hand to Southerners, for the carpetbaggers were only just beginning to lose their deadly grip on the South.

His Enfield rifle, one he had captured on the field of battle, was clean and loaded, in a rack in the corner. He also owned a Frontier Model Colt six-shooter and it now reposed in its holster on the bench. He had removed the heavy belt for comfort.

The old fellow's first warning of danger was the sudden kicking open of his plank door. It flew back on its leather hinges and vibrated for a moment as the bottom stuck on a high point in the board flooring. Startled, Styles brought his feet down and started to jump up but the man bulking in the doorway stopped him.

6

"Sit still, Styles," the man said gruffly.

Styles smelled deadly trouble. He was too shrewd a judge of men not to see that his visitor was dangerous and that there were more men of the same kind hurrying up. He waited, his pistol a few feet away from him.

"What yuh want?" he demanded. "There's some coffee left in the pot. Put her on the stove, feller. Yuh savvy my name but I don't know yores."

"Nobody else around, Dowie," reported one of the shadows outside. "All clear."

"My handle is Dowie Burke," said the tough in the door.

Styles studied him. The man had a bulldog jaw darkened by beard stubble, and black eyes smoldered deep in his skull. His mouth was twisted and under his Stetson showed curly dark hair which needed cutting.

A leather jacket and scratched chaps over blue pants tucked into run-over half-boots, a sweated shirt and red bandanna made up his apparel. At his waist rode crossed gun-belts and open holsters for the two heavy pistols.

Dowie Burke was burly and large of frame, and his hands were square and hamlike. It was obvious that he had tremendous physical strength and endurance.

He just stood there, regarding old Styles who tried to dissemble. Styles wanted to get hold of his pistol and hitched his stool around but Dowie Burke said instantly:

"None of that."

"What is it?" asked Styles again.

It took nerve not to panic under Burke's threatening stare. Death was in the little cabin and Lon Styles knew it. Any instant these men would kill. He had been in too many dangerous spots not to sense it.

"Small place, but it will have to do, boys," remarked Burke coldly.

Burke's heavy right hand moved and Styles tried to save himself in a last desperate fling. He threw himself across the table and grasped his pistol. The rickety table tilted off the lamp and sent it crashing to the floor but before the light was doused Burke had drawn and fired into Styles' side. The Confederate major caught two heavy bullets in the ribs and was dying as the table turned over and threw him to the floor.

"Strike a match, Nifty," ordered Dowie Burke.

They righted the lamp and lighted it. The chimney had been cracked but it gave enough illumination to see Lon Styles lying there, breathing his last. Styles had kept a hold on his gun and died with it in his hand.

The men with Burke were of the same mold, dressed, as they were, in leather and Stetsons; roughs of the range. Some were lean, others stout and short, but each had the expression of a man who lives in evil ways. They were armed with carbines, six-shooters, and knives.

"Jack, go tell Tynsdale to come in," commanded Dowie Burke, as he bent over Styles and began to rifle the dead man's pockets.

After a few minutes two more men pushed into the cabin.

"Send your boys outside, Dowie," ordered the man in the lead.

Burke and these two men remained in the shack and the door was closed.

Sidney Tynsdale, the man who had given Burke orders, was plainly the man's superior. He was in his middle thirties, ten years older than Dowie Burke, but it was not a matter of years. Burke looked up to Tynsdale and offered him a henchman's subservience, the attitude of a less experienced rascal toward a cleverer, more deadly one.

Tynsdale's eyes had the cold aspect of blue marbles. The flesh stretched taut over his protruding cheekbones, touched by small red blotches of broken veins that told of high living. He had a predatory nose and thin lips, and his mustache and beard were brownish in hue.

He wore riding clothes but the black leather was new

8

and clean, unlike that of Burke and his men. His black hat had a narrow brim and his boots had recently been polished though yellowish dust clung to them. He unbuttoned his jacket and raised a fine white hand, a large diamond catching the light from the ring setting on his middle finger. He was proud of his hands although they were small for a man, feminine in their veined whiteness.

Tynsdale sat down on the stool which Burke set straight for him, drumming sharply on the table top with two fingers of his right hand. For a moment he silently regarded Dowie Burke who shifted uneasily under the steady scrutiny.

"*Jacta est alea,*" he said then. "That means the die is cast, Burke. You have proved yourself to me."

"Yes suh." Burke nodded, and seemed relieved. "I told yuh I'd carry out any orders yuh give me."

The man in a simple black suit and hat who had entered with Tynsdale stood silently by the closed door. He was a slim man whose sharp dark face showed he was of Spanish extraction. His shoulders were bowed, his dark eyes were set in pits, and his lips curved in a gloomy expression. Yellowish hands stuck from scanty sleeves too short for the elongated arms. He had a serpentine aspect and his noiseless, alert manner accentuated the impression.

"Hold the door, Palacio," Tynsdale ordered him, nodding.

Palacio heard and obeyed, but gave no sign or word in response.

Dowie Burke knew that Felipe Palacio was Tynsdale's bodyguard and Man Friday, that Tynsdale was seldom seen without his shadow. The slimy, creepy way that Palacio moved and behaved worried Burke. It was unlike anything he had come up against and Burke had consorted with the dregs of humanity in the Southwest.

Palacio carried a stiletto as sharp as a needle, and long enough to pierce a man's body. He was never without at

9

least two pistols, one in a shoulder holster and a small one in his coat pocket. Burke was convinced that Palacio was utterly devoted to Tynsdale and would kill at Tynsdale's slightest signal, and it made him uneasy.

Still, Burke had thrown in with Tynsdale and so Palacio should be on Burke's side of the fence. Yet Palacio's attitude was of unbending, single-minded attention to Tynsdale. His eyes burned with a fanatical glow and Burke was well aware that, while he was obsequious to the point of servility with the man who was virtually his master that he treated others with open contempt, not noticing them unless something about them concerned Tynsdale. Then Palacio was ready to spring.

The man who had owned the cabin was dead. Lon Styles was stiffening on the uneven floor. Tynsdale glanced at the corpse and murmured:

"*Caput mortuum.*"

"What's that, suh?" inquired Burke, awed and impressed by Tynsdale's superior talents.

"It means worthless remains, Dowie. You will bury them in one of the brush-choked cuts I noticed on the way here."

Tynsdale deliberately unbuttoned his black coat to get at his inside pocket. As the coat parted a heavy gold chain showed over his paunch and a solitaire diamond glinted from the fob. He brought out a case and placed spectacles on the high bridge of his nose. He drew forth a folded sheet of paper and flattened it out on the table before him, pulling the lamp closer to it.

Tynsdale's fingers rapped sharply, three little thuds with his forefingers, two with the middle. Palacio immediately turned and yanked the door open. A couple of Burke's toughs were almost against it, plainly eavesdropping.

"I want your men to stay away till we're through, Dowie," Tynsdale said to Dowie Burke.

10

He was not angry, but rather was pleased with his own acumen.

"Keep off, cuss yuh," growled Dowie angrily to the men outside.

They drew away and Palacio closed the door and stood before it. Burke realized then that Tynsdale's tappings had meant something, at least to Palacio.

"Look at this," ordered Tynsdale.

Burke stepped closer and saw the paper held by Tynsdale's white hand. There were several names written in a round, even fashion, each letter scrupulously formed. The first name was "Lon Styles." Tynsdale took out a jeweled pencil and then drew a careful line through Styles' name.

Dowie Burke's sullen lips moved as he read the next name. It was "Moss Jordan—Nod Hill Farm."

There were more names below that of Jordan.

Burke waited and Tynsdale explained.

"These are the men who are in my way, Dowie. You've proved yourself to me by getting rid of Styles. Go on from here. You can use this place as a headquarters while you operate in the vicinity. Keep my name out of it, of course. I have money for you tonight and you'll be well paid as we go along, with a big bonus at the end. Be careful. Work quietly so the law won't interfere. We can handle the county sheriff and local officers but we want to skip the Rangers if we can."

Tynsdale had a map of the Yellow Hills country and gave precise and valuable instructions to Dowie Burke. He paid Burke with a bag of money. When Tynsdale had finished he took off his spectacles and a smile deepened the creases about his eyes.

"*Decrevi*—I have decreed, Dowie," he murmured.

"Yes, suh. Yuh'll find I do things to suit yuh."

Burke put the folded list in his shirt pocket and fastened the button.

11

Tynsdale rose and Palacio tensed the way a dog does when its master moves. The two went out and rode away, leaving Dowie Burke and his men at Styles' cabin.

CHAPTER II

Buzzards In The Sky

Ben Naler, virile young cowman from the Trans-Pecos, felt his heart lilt with happy anticipation as he rode up and dismounted in front of Moss Jordan's ranchhouse. Naler was a tall and sinewy young fellow with curly, copper-colored hair, and uncommonly straight-looking blue eyes. His skin, cleanly shaven, was bronzed from sun and wind of the wilderness. He had put on a new blue shirt and a clean bandanna before leaving Stuart's Ford, the little town on the river where he had taken a room.

Naler dropped his reins, and his long legs, clad in chaps, blue pants, and half-boots with silver spurs, took him slowly toward the shaded veranda of the house. Out back were long stables and corrals. In them were the beautiful Kentucky horses which had first brought him to Moss Jordan's place.

Naler had come then from his big ranch to buy blooded stock with which he hoped to improve the mustang breed of his own mounts. Left to themselves, mustangs grew scrawny and smaller as they ran in a wild state. Tough as they might be they needed more size.

There were a couple of men working around the stables but Naler did not see Moss Jordan there. He gave a whistle and halloa and presently Jordan came through the house and outside.

"Why, howdy, Naler," he greeted.

Jordan, a wiry man of medium height, strong and active, had been a Confederate cavalry officer and had fought under such famous Southern generals as Stonewall Jackson and Jeb Stuart. He had been wounded twice in action. After the War he had taken the oath of allegiance to the United States as the law had required all ex-Confederate officers to do, but had promptly left his impoverished Kentucky plantation and emigrated to Texas, where he had settled on the Colorado among the Yellow Hills.

He had saved a few stallions and mares of the fine strain his family had owned and brought them to Texas, where he hoped to build up a big horse farm. But as yet he had none for sale, and when Ben Naler had first approached him, he had refused to let any go. He was trying to get a backlog of breeders before he cashed in on excess stock.

It was three days since Naler had made his first visit, and the young cowman felt self-conscious in Jordan's presence. He wondered if Moss Jordan could see through him.

"I come back, Mr. Jordan," he said. "Figgered yuh might have changed yore mind about the hosses."

Jordan's thick, graying eyebrows drew together, and his sharp face took on lines indicative of a peppery disposition. That was emphasized by his quick way of talking. His career as a colonel had given him a habit of command, and he could judge a man. Keen gray eyes now fixed Naler who shifted a bit.

"Why no, son," Jordan said, with deceptive mildness. "I ain't changed my mind. I told yuh I wanted to build up my string before I sell any hosses. Mebbe in a year or two I could let yuh have some."

Moss Jordan's bearded face was set. Naler dropped his gaze, feeling embarrassed. But he looked up quickly as a

13

girl's voice called: "Why, hello, Mr. Naler. You back so soon?"

In the front doorway stood smiling Connie Jordan, Moss' daughter, whose golden hair and amber eyes held a magic for men. She was small but exquisitely formed—and she was the real reason why Ben Naler had been drawn back to Jordan's.

Naler felt all hands and feet, as awkward as a scarecrow. He was confused, as he thought that both Connie and Moss would guess why he had returned. Jordan had been positive in his refusal to sell any horses, and nobody but a fool would have come again so soon.

But Jordan had not banked on Connie. A widower who had lost his wife during the awful war, he took the girl more or less for granted. Connie kept house for her father and his two aides.

Just as Naler thought he would melt into the ground with embarrassment, Connie came to his rescue.

"Come on in and stay for dinner, Mr. Naler," she invited cordially.

"Yes, ma'am." Naler was glad to pass Moss who was still watching him.

Jordan scratched his head. "Oh," he said. "I'll be there in a jiffy, Connie." He went on around the house.

The house was small but comfortably furnished and there were the signs of a woman's influence all around— in the curtains at the window, the flowers on the table and the cleanliness. The odor of the food was appetizing, too. Naler, a young bachelor, lived alone in his cow kingdom and it was just such things that brought him to a realization of what he was missing. And there was, of course, Connie herself.

"I wish yuh'd make it Ben, ma'am," he told her, as he took off his hat inside.

"All right, Ben," she said lightly. "And I'm Connie, you know. Excuse me while I see to the roast. I don't want it to burn."

14

In a little while Naler ate with the Jordans and the two hands. The meal was excellent, with home-baked bread and freshly churned butter. But Ben Naler was hardly aware of anything except the proximity of the girl. He had been ceaselessly thinking about her since he had met her and had been unable to rest until he got back to her.

One of Jordan's hired men was a smiling, young fellow, and Naler watched him jealously, wondering if Connie and he might be interested in one another. Connie smiled at them all.

"I'm worried, mighty worried," Jordan was saying when the meal was drawing to a close. "What do yuh say we ride over to Lon's after dinner, Connie?"

"All right," she agreed. "It's a nice day. Just the same you oughtn't to be worried about Uncle Lon, Dad. You know how he is. He probably was too busy to ride over yesterday."

"He knew we'd have chicken and dumplin's for dinner," insisted her father. "He never failed to come on Sunday before."

"What's wrong?" asked Naler, for a moment withdrawing his attention from the girl.

"Oh, an old friend of father's named Lon Styles usually comes to Sunday dinner," Connie explained. "They play checkers and fight the War over again. He didn't show up yesterday."

Naler paid scant attention. He was in a thrall of enchantment with Connie present. He was relieved when the young hired man went out, back to work at the stables. He helped Connie clean up and she smiled at him and seemed pleased and decidedly friendly.

Moss Jordan had his own and Connie's horse saddled when Naler and the girl left the kitchen.

"Let's ride," sang out Jordan.

Connie changed her clothes and came out wearing a brown riding dress and a short-sleeved knitted jacket.

15

She had a small hat on her golden hair. She was breathtakingly beautiful, thought Naler.

Moss Jordan rode ahead, crossing the river on a narrow wooden bridge and taking a trail into the brushy hills. Naler rode beside Connie and answered her questions. She was keenly interested in ranching.

"I wish father would move out there where you are," she said. "It must be wonderful."

"It's nice in some ways," agreed Naler. "But it's mighty lonesome at times." He flushed a bit as he realized what he had said and wondered if Connie would think he was bold. "I mean there ain't many neighbors like around here, ma'am. Yuh go it alone out there." He was eager to appear before her in the best light, for he felt humble before her beauty.

The sun was warm. As they climbed the slanting, rocky trail, the hoofs of the horses kicked up yellowish dust. But the time sped much too fast to suit Ben Naler, in Connie's company and though it was several miles to Styles' place, they sighted it too soon to suit Naler. And as they saw the shack nestling between the hills, they saw some saddle horses outside it.

"Huh—looks like he's got visitors," said Jordan, surprised.

Several men stood around outside the cabin watching them as they approached. One of them stepped forward to greet them as they drew rein. He was a tough-looking fellow, thought Ben Naler. He had a bulldog jaw and hot black eyes, and Colts rode in his oiled holsters. Naler had had experience with rustlers and fugitives from justice who swarmed in the lawless land across the Pecos and he would have said at once that the burly man was dangerous, if not outlaw.

"Well, what can I do for yuh?" demanded the heavy-set stranger.

"Where's Lon Styles?" asked Jordan. "I'm a pard of his.

16

Missed him when he didn't show up yesterday at my place."

"Oh. Yuh're a friend of Styles, huh?"

Naler didn't fancy the sneering attitude of the heavy-set man. He was angry but he only watched, allowing Jordan to handle the situation.

Jordan's eyes narrowed. "Where is Styles?" he said shortly.

The thickness in the air could fairly be felt. Then the burly man broke the silence.

"He's my uncle," he said, more politely. "My handle is Burke. I'm Styles' nephew and come for a visit. Yuh see he wanted to take a run to New Orleans so he done left me in charge here while he's away."

Naler had an eye on the armed toughs slouched against the house wall. Burke watched Jordan, who was scowling.

"I'm Moss Jordan, Burke," the former Kentuckian said. "Styles and I are like brothers. I never heard him speak of yuh."

"Yuh ain't callin' me a liar, I hope?" Burke said softly.

Connie was alarmed. Moss Jordan had a quick fighting temper and it was flaring up. She edged her horse close to her father's and put a hand on his arm.

"Oh, Father, your memory's terrible," she cried brightly. "I remember Uncle Lon speaking of Mr. Burke . . . It's late. We've got to get on home."

"Huh." Jordan set his jaw, but as Connie pulled at him he wheeled his mount and started off.

Naler and Connie followed and they left the cabin behind, Burke and his friends eying them until they had turned around the bluff.

Then Moss exploded. "What do yuh make of that!"

"What's wrong?" inquired Naler.

"Why, that feller's no relation of Lon's," said Jordan.

"Father, that man's dangerous!" broke in Connie.

17

Both were distressed and Naler sympathized. It was a mystery, and Jordan swore he would clear it up.

They took the trail for home, over the hill. A couple of miles from Styles' cabin Naler spoke of something which his keen sight had noted for some time. He had a far-seeing eye and an attention for details which came from his life in the wilderness.

"Buzzards over there, Mr. Jordan."

Specks wheeled and dropped from the azure sky. Moss Jordan thought enough of it to leave the trail in spite of Connie's fears. Naler and the girl followed and after about a mile of twisting in and out over rocky terrain spotted with clumps of woods and bush, they reached the point where Naler had spied the vultures. The big birds flew up, screeching at the interruption, and growls and yelps sounded as a pack of mongrel dogs bristled and snarled at them.

Jordan drew his pistol and cocked it, firing a shot. The animals turned and fled, yelping.

"They're bad as wolves," explained Moss. "They come from homeless dogs durin' the War and they've gone wild. Tear yuh to pieces if they get yuh down."

Up the cut they found what they were hunting. It was the body of Lon Styles, Jordan's old friend. The buzzards and dogs had worried and dug it out of the yellow dirt where Styles had been buried under loose earth and rocks.

Moss Jordan was deeply saddened. He knelt by the remains of his crony, mourning for Styles.

"Poor Lon! Cuss it, he had a lonely life of it. Lost his folks in the war, and now he's gone!"

Naler was more practical, for he did not have the personal sense of bereavement.

"Somebody shot him through the ribs, Mr. Jordan," he pointed out. "Then they brought the body out and buried it here."

Something plugged into the earth not a foot from Moss Jordan, and Connie gave a quick scream.

"Come on—that was a heavy rifle bullet!" cried Naler.

He grasped Connie and lifted her to her saddle, then helped Jordan up. Moss Jordan was furious.

"I'll go back there and have it out with that Burke rascal!" he howled.

"Look, there's a dozen of 'em comin'," said the cooler Naler. "And we got Connie along."

The burly man they had met at Styles' cabin was indeed coming at them, with his followers.

"Up that way—hustle!" ordered Naler, indicating a path around the cut which would take them around the rise and put some protection between them and Burke. "Take care of Connie!"

He dropped back, Colt in hand, turned in his saddle and began firing at Burke who was working the rifle. He could hear the singing slugs in the air and a couple kicked up shale and dirt too close for comfort.

Naler slowly retreated around the bend. He could see Moss Jordan and the girl riding down a long slope which would eventually bring them to safety. He went on for a time and again swung to blast the turn as Burke and his toughs pushed up.

Fighting a clever delaying action, Ben Naler gave his friends time to escape. Then Moss Jordan dropped back, when Connie was well out ahead, and sent bullets at the enemy.

Burke was dogged, though, and evidently infuriated because they had uncovered Styles' body. He kept pressing after them, hoping to pick off Naler and Jordan. Then he would capture the girl!

19

CHAPTER III

Texas Calls

Captain William McDowell, Chief of Texas Rangers at Austin, paced his office floor with the same equanimity a freshly caged tiger might display. Not that McDowell would literally bite any hand thrust too close, but he did feel like it.

This was due to a combination of circumstances, all of which had long annoyed the old officer. And superimposed on the festering sores of the past years had come a new call from Texas to the Rangers for help. The wire had reached McDowell that morning and it was from a point not a hundred miles southeast of the capital.

"That's gettin' plumb close to home," thought McDowell irately.

Bill McDowell had been a star Ranger in his younger days and had brought in or left lying more than his share of outlaws, Indians and other enemies of the Lone Star State. He still stood six feet but he was partially crippled with the ills of old age and could no longer leap to his mustang and be off to the wars.

He was too valuable a man to be retired, however, with his shrewd understanding of human nature and the particular problems of Texas. So from his Austin headquarters, McDowell was responsible for law enforcement in vast areas and he managed it with a handful of men. Even though Texas, impoverished by the Civil War, was a gigantic problem, since the state was just beginning to heave her mighty self out of the mire of defeat and the carpetbagger regime.

20

Though he could not answer this touching appeal himself there was more than one way to skin a cougar in the old Ranger Captain's opinion. McDowell had come to his decision and as usual he acted at once upon it. He happened to be across the room from his desk where his call bell stood but he was pulling on a cold pipe. He took it from his clenched teeth and hurled it at the bell, making a bull's-eye, since he was an excellent shot with any variety of weapon.

A clerk with the startled look of a surprised rabbit peeked in the door.

"Send Ranger Hatfield in!" roared McDowell. "Then go out and buy me a new pipe. These newfangled ones don't last a man any time at all. Look at that! It busted into four pieces."

He kicked the broken pipe under the desk and folded his arms, staring out the window and trying to contain himself. Then he heard a soft step and a pleasant, drawling voice said:

"Good mornin', Cap'n Bill."

McDowell turned. It was always a comfort to see Jim Hatfield, his greatest Ranger.

Hatfield impressed the beholder at once. He stood well over six feet, with long, powerful legs cased in leather riding pants. His shoulders pushed out the dark shirt he wore and his body tapered to the narrow hips of the lithe fighting man. Here depended the big Colt revolvers in supple holsters equipped with rawhide thongs to hold them in position when riding or running.

Hatfield was too rugged to be called handsome. That was a weak word to describe the leashed might and rippling strength in him. The sun and winds of the wild trails had bronzed him a golden hue. The strap of his big Stetson was loose in the runner and framed his determined jaw. Though he carried himself easily, now in repose, those slender hands could draw and fire the Colts with stunning speed. His gray-green eyes, so lazy, in anger could grow as cold as dark ice. His wide mouth broke the severity of his face.

McDowell knew that Jim Hatfield had an unbreakable nerve in battle, the hickory and coiled lightning and skill to back it up. And to make Hatfield practically indispensable to McDowell and the State the tall officer had a quick mind which could size up and accurately judge a situation.

Some men were clever but did not have the physical stamina to win; others had brute strength and a ruthless bull way of boring in but made mistakes in strategy and tactics. But Jim Hatfield, modest as his manner was, possessed both brains and fighting ability of the first caliber.

"Sit down," ordered McDowell, and Hatfield complied.

Blue clouds of tobacco smoke idled from the quirly he was smoking as he listened to McDowell.

The captain spread the telegram that had so disturbed him before the Ranger. Hatfield could read it at a glance but McDowell felt impelled to talk it out:

"Signed Colonel Moss Jordan," he said. "I think he fought under Jeb Stuart and mebbe Jackson too. Anyway I'm sick of the way ex-officers of the Confederacy been put upon even when they done took the oath. There's been a killin' in the Yellow Hills, not a hundred miles southeast of here on the Colorado."

Hatfield nodded. He knew something of the section under discussion, for he had passed through it on his way to the Gulf Coast. Austin itself stood on the upper Colorado.

"Goldy and I can make it in a day, suh," Hatfield said. said.

"*Bueno*. I think yuh better hurry. The killin' was that of Major Lon Styles and yuh see Jordan says Styles was an old Army pard. Look around careful, Hatfield. Texas is just beginnin' to rid herself of the carpetbaggers who have persecuted these former Confederates.

"Styles is dead, but yuh might be able to save Jordan

22

and others. Jordan seems to think he's in danger of death and evidently there's a tough bunch operatin' in his vicinity. 'Dowie Burke.' I think I had complaints on an hombre with that handle from the Border and other parts."

Hatfield memorized what information McDowell had for him. He could smell danger and sense the urgency of Jordan's appeal to the Rangers. The killers were after Moss Jordan and even now he might be finished, before Hatfield could make it. The big map of Texas on the office wall showed that a small settlement called Stuart's Ford was the nearest town to Jordan's place.

The Ranger was glad to be moving. He did not like cities but preferred the lonely wilderness trails and the thrills brought by conflict with enemies of the State. McDowell shook hands and wished him luck and the old Captain meant it.

"I don't know what I'd do if he didn't come back from a job," mused McDowell, as he watched the big Ranger approach the magnificent golden sorrel awaiting him outside.

Goldy was Hatfield's friend and partner. The gelding had wonderful endurance and strength, a speed which had carried Hatfield out of many ticklish situations. A carbine rode in a sling under one long leg of the mighty rider as Hatfield mounted and turned to wave goodby from the saddle.

The Colts rode at Hatfield's bunched hips and he had spare shells in the belt loops. He carried extra ammunition, iron rations, water, and at the cantle was a neat roll containing a poncho, blanket and a few more necessities. He could live off the country if need be and so was not limited in his maneuvers. . . .

The following afternoon found Hatfield in Stuart's Ford. The sleepy little settlement reposed on the south bank of the Colorado. It was vital that the sorrel have rest and a real feed, and besides the Ranger desired to check up on the town and get information as to the exact location of Moss Jordan's. Also there might be gossip as to Styles' death and the killers who had descended on the section.

Hatfield first saw to Goldy's needs and after a rubdown and a small drink for the sorrel he left his mount in a corral behind the livery stable.

He walked up the awning-shaded way. A glance completely took in Stuart's Ford. Main Street was the one real street, running on both sides of the plaza. There was a general store called Hillary's, three saloons, one of good size and advertising rooms to rent. There was also a blacksmith shop, the livery, a hardware store specializing in firearms and ammunition, and few more buildings made up the place.

Stuart's Ford had a shabby but virtuous air as though it had settled for a nap in the warm sunshine by the river and did not desire to be disturbed. Such a spot might boast a day constable and a night watchman, but for real law enforcement must depend on a county sheriff. As many of these encumbents at the time had been placed in office by the carpetbaggers who had taken advantage of the disfranchised Texans, it was a tossup whether the sheriff would be a help or a hindrance. In any case, the county seat was twenty miles away.

There were a few saddle horses as well as farm wagons standing at the railings separating the sidewalks from the yellow street. This was a mixed community of small ranches, farms and homes nestling in the Yellow Hills. There were no really big cowmen such as governed the empire of the Trans-Pecos and south Texas but their people were citizens of the Lone Star commonwealth and entitled to protection.

Low hills were covered with brush and patches of woods. The Colorado valley cut through these with innumerable nicks and indentations, made at a time long ago

24

when the stream was wild and jumped its banks with regularity.

The Gulf lay a day's ride farther east, with the rapidly growing city of Houston east by north. Where the Gulf plains began so did the cotton growing, but around the Yellow Hills there were no such plantations.

Hatfield was hungry, thirsty and tired. He strode to the largest of the saloons which rented rooms, the Palace Hotel & Bar. He had a drink, ordered a meal and paid for a bed.

It was a feat to enter a strange town and get any real information, but the Ranger was trained at such work. He did not show any curiosity but began chatting with the barkeeper at the Palace. There were a few customers down the bar. Before long, without his informant suspecting what he was after, Hatfield knew the exact location of Moss Jordan's place, where Lon Styles had lived and what the town thought about it all.

He did not wish to move, however, until Goldy was rested. A jaded horse might spell ruin and death. So the Ranger ate his hot meal and though it was broad daylight went upstairs to the bare little cubicle which contained a cot and a table. He lay down and slept. . . .

Night had fallen when the tall Ranger quietly saddled Goldy and set out for Jordan's place. There was a road meandering through the river valley, skirting natural obstructions above high-water mark. Jordan's was said to be on the same side as Stuart's Ford, while Lon Styles had dwelt north of the stream.

The Yellow Hills loomed about him, their summits touched by the rising moon. It had cooled a bit with the setting of the sun but it was still warm. He could hear the slow murmur of the Colorado to his right and occasionally see a stretch of the silvery water. As he moved upriver he sighted here and there the small lights of some habitation.

His imagination carried him inside these homes. There

would be men and women, and children. Supper would be over and they would be resting after the day's labor, peaceful and snug at home. At night all houses looked inviting, cozy, mused Hatfield.

The west wind puffed dust into his eyes and he turned his chin down and shook his head. Goldy had brought him well away from the settlement and the Ranger, cleaning his eyes of particles, looked ahead once again. He sighted lighted windows in the river valley some distance on. The road hugged an undercut cliff and he was against its darkness.

The golden sorrel shivered and slowed without any knee pressure. He sniffed softly, giving warning to his rider.

Immediately Hatfield drew up and sat his saddle with ear cocked. Goldy had told him that someone or something was moving up there, and natural caution kept the Ranger from blundering on in the darkness.

CHAPTER IV

Surprise for a Drygulcher

Hatfield waited, as patient as Fate. But he knew that the animal senses of his horse were keener than any man's could be, and that some scent had reached Goldy's flared nostrils, brought on the warm wind.

At last he was rewarded as he caught the sounds of splashing. They came from the river and were upstream. He decided that men must be crossing the Colorado from the north bank.

He moved on a bit, hunting a possible niche in the cliff into which to retire in case they came his way. Again he pulled up, pressing back and freezing. The horsemen were coming up the slope onto the road and he saw a cigarette glow ruby red in a man's mouth as the smoker dragged on it. Voices reached him.

"Douse that quirly and keep shut," an irritated command was snapped out. "Yuh want Jordan to savvy yuh're comin'?"

The cigarette was put out after a final inhalation. The dark figures swung up the river road away from the Ranger. He was not certain how many were in the party but he guessed ten or a dozen. Allowing them a lead he followed in the dust kicked up by the trotting horses.

The mention of Jordan had alerted the Ranger. The colonel who had sent his complaint to McDowell had mentioned that he was in personal danger.

They left their horses some distance out from a lighted house which Hatfield was certain was Moss Jordan's home. He could see two windows in front, a couple more at the side. Two holders were left with the mustangs to keep them quiet as the others started quietly toward Jordan's.

The Ranger dismounted and patted Goldy's neck. The sorrel would stand and wait in the shadows of the brush clump until Hatfield whistled or came for him.

Expert as an Apache Indian at such work, the tall officer flitted in. He circled the spot where the mustangs restlessly pawed and sniffed, and heard the low talk of the holders. It was too dark to see much of the surroundings, but Hatfield could make out that the area about the buildings was cleared but that there were patches of woods and brush not far away. The stealthy attackers used this cover as they crept forward.

Hatfield was flat against the earth from time to time, listening intently. He could hear men moving in a small grove of trees to his left. He could not see them at all now and the faint noises seemed thin for so many men so he froze behind a jutting tongue of rock, a great boulder half buried in the earth.

The progress of someone in the woods was checked and then resumed. Hatfield caught a few words.

"They got a sentry on the porch, Dowie," a man was reporting. "I seen his gun barrel when he shifted."

Hatfield decided that the main bunch had waited while a scout went to the edge of the woods to spy on Jordan's. "Dowie" could well be Dowie Burke, the outlaw named in the complaint.

Another speaker's voice reached the keen ears of the Texas Ranger. He thought it the same as the gruff one which had cautioned the riders back on the road.

"Give me that new Sharps," ordered the hidden man. "I'm goin' to crawl over to that rock and lie there and see what I can hit. If they got a guard out there's no chance of rushin' in, but mebbe I can pick off Jordan and Naler. You boys stick here and keep it quiet. Cover me."

Hatfield lay squeezed against the opposite side of the rock. He could hear the creeping enemy crossing from the woods to the boulder. He was ready, but the man stopped on the near edge of the rock and set himself there.

The Ranger sought to control his breathing. It seemed to him that it must be extra loud but he could not hear the fellow on the other side, except when the latter moved himself. By raising his eyes Hatfield could see the side windows. Through one showed an oil lamp burning on the table and a woman's figure passed between the window and light. Then a man went by, moving in the front of the house.

Hatfield heard the throaty *cluck-cluck* of the cocking Sharps. A man again was silhouetted against that light now and paused at the table to pick up something, a newspaper or magazine. This made that person inside a sitting duck target for an expert marksman, and Hatfield gathered himself to spring.

The lithe Ranger vaulted the boulder and landed with both feet in the small of the back of the prostrate drygulcher there. The Sharps went off with a deafening roar and glass tinkled. A woman inside the house screamed shrilly in terror and a man began shouting.

Hatfield had wrecked the drygulcher's aim but he quickly found he had caught a Tartar. The man's heavy rifle barrel slashed at him and nearly cracked his left forearm as the fellow cursed frantically. The Ranger slipped his vise grip to the warm steel of the barrel and with a wrench ripped the Sharps away and flung it aside. But in this moment his enemy got to his knees and slugged him in the solar plexus with a terrific punch.

It was a paralyzing blow and the Ranger nearly lost his life as the killer whipped out a Colt and threw it up. But with a superhuman effort Jim Hatfield threw himself forward. The pistol roared in his ear and he felt the burn of flashing powder against his cheek. The bullet missed him by a breath and with all his skill the Ranger slid a hand from the gun wrist and closed his fingers on the cylinder. The Colt could not be fired again while he held on.

He brought up a knee and his adversary grunted in pain. Hatfield's ears still rang with the explosion of the gun and his heart pumped blood at a frantic rate, making his ears hum. He was dimly aware of yells and calls from both house and the woods where this killer had left his companions. But such things were only vague, for Hatfield was totally engrossed in the conflict.

He bored in and the bending of his foe's arm forced the man to let go of the Colt and try to turn so his bone would not be snapped by the pressure. Suddenly the man under him fell back and carried the tall officer along with him. Hatfield landed on top but was slugged in the nose with such force that his eyes watered.

Grunts, curses and whistling breath told him that the drygulcher was in as bad if not worse condition than he was himself, as Hatfield slowly but surely gained the upper hand. Actually only seconds had elapsed since he had jumped his man, but it seemed they had been battling a long time.

The noises in his ears abated and so did the shock of the first clash. Hatfield heard men in the trees calling:

"Dowie! Dowie! What's wrong? Come on!"

A gunshot banged from the direction of the house as the sentry let one go at the noises and the spot where he had seen the Sharps flame. A bullet whizzed over Hatfield and Dowie as they struggled on the sandy dirt.

Hatfield was bringing his right fist up and down with the sturdy insistence of a triphammer, landing on Dowie's face each time and trying to hold the man down with his weight and his left arm. Dowie was as slippery as a greased pig, and he could take a lot of punishment. He never quit struggling and he began to shriek:

"This way, boys! This way!"

The Ranger was aware of a rush from the woods. The riders who had come here with Dowie were entering the fight. It would mean death. He was sure Dowie had another gun in his holsters, and he wanted to disable the man enough so that Dowie could not kill him when he turned. He quit punching Dowie and got a grip on Dowie's shirt front, meaning to throw him over.

Heavy as Dowie was, the Ranger picked him off the earth and started to hurl him away. But the shirt front was rotted and ripped in the Ranger's grip. The whip of it sent Dowie reeling toward his followers who had almost reached him, but dared not fire into the melee for fear of killing their leader.

The sudden release of Dowie's weight sent Hatfield staggering back and his heels caught in a low rock shelf. He fell back, bruised against the sharp side of the boulder, but still unconsciously holding most of Dowie's shirt front in his hand.

Dark figures were dashing at him from the woods. Dowie was rolling over and over toward the oncoming men and yelling to them at the top of his lungs:

"Kill him! Kill that hombre over there, boys!"

Revolvers blared and lead spattered against the stone. Hatfield flipped himself around and scrabbled over the top of the big rock. He dropped the cloth he had been gripping as though for dear life and drew a Colt.

He would have shot Dowie then but the others were around their chief. Dowie was frantically trying to tell them what had occurred and pointing at the boulder. Bullets hunted for the tall Ranger as he crouched behind his shield. He bobbed up to shoot and his bullets sent them streaking back into the woods, Dowie with them. But one man threw up his hands and crashed with a howl before he could reach shelter.

The Ranger dusted the brush, his lead spaced in the trees. He was breathing hard from exertion and his back and arm hurt. He tried to judge where they were by the cracklings made as they retreated toward their mustangs, but gunfire opened behind him. Men from the house had circled and the light in the building had been put out.

A bullet smacked into the rock on Hatfield's side, sent by the very men he had come to help. They could not distinguish friend from foe in the night and were excited by the attempted drygulching.

"Hold it, Jordan!" bawled the Ranger, edging to the side of the rocks.

A hard and determined voice answered him.

"Who's that? Speak up or I'll blow yore head off."

"Don't shoot!" called the Ranger. "I'm a friend!"

"Yeah?" replied the voice, a sarcastic note in it. "Do friends shoot an hombre through the window?"

There was no more shooting from the woods. Dowie and his men had fled except for the silent figure lying face down a few yards from the trees.

"I didn't fire that shot," argued Hatfield. "Listen and

yuh'll hear Dowie and his boys ridin' off. It was Dowie tried to drygulch yuh and I stopped him."

There was a silence. The Ranger, crouched by the boulder, could hear men all around him, aware each had a bead on him. The beat of retreating hoofs helped win the argument for the Ranger.

"If yuh're a friend come out with yore hands reachin'!" another voice called. "Steady, now."

"Here I come!" the officer called back.

He stood up and put up his hands, slowly walking into the open space. He had made about twenty paces when the hard voice ordered:

"Now stop and let us have a look at yuh."

Hatfield complied. A man rose from behind his elbow and came carefully closer, a carbine raised and cocked. The Ranger could see him out of the corner of his eye. He was a tall, lean fellow. A shorter figure jumped up at Hatfield's left and bored in, covering him.

"All right, Naler," said the second man who had spoken. There was a commanding ring in his voice. "Get in behind him and lift his guns."

As the tall man moved nearer Hatfield now could see a couple more armed aides.

"Yuh're losin' time," Hatfield assured. "Dowie and his men are way off by now. Are you Moss Jordan?"

"What yuh want with him?" the smaller man asked suspiciously.

"I come out to talk with Moss Jordan," explained the Ranger. "Yuh savvy Cap'n McDowell? I bumped into a dozen drygulchers and trailed 'em here. Had a scrap with one who tried for yuh from this rock when yuh showed in front of the light."

CHAPTER V

Death List

Evidently the tall man was Naler, for it was he who came up behind the Ranger and snatched the Colts from his holsters. Hatfield let his guns go for he had a spare hidden under his shirt, and he knew he must identify himself to these men anyway.

The mention of McDowell impressed the man who must be Moss Jordan.

"McDowell!" he exclaimed. "Yuh mean yuh're from Austin?"

"Yes suh."

"I'm Moss Jordan," the horse rancher said promptly. "Well, come on into the house and we'll talk it over."

"Better check up outside first, Jordan," advised Hatfield. "I shot one of 'em when they run for the woods."

"Rob, fetch a lantern!" ordered Jordan.

One of the men padded toward the barn.

"Father!" a woman's voice filled with anxiety called. "Ben! Are you all right?"

"Yeah, we're fine!" shouted back Moss Jordan.

Presently Rob brought a lighted lantern. The yellow rays showed the mighty Ranger's rugged features, his size, and his fighting look. He was bruised and his clothing dirty from the set-to with Dowie, but Moss Jordan gave a quick whistle at sight of him.

"They didn't spare the materials when they made yuh, did they, mister?"

Hatfield nodded. He was used to comments on his size. He lowered his hands.

"Could we have a word in private, Jordan?" he said. "Send yore men away a bit."

Jordan nodded and waved the other three men off.

"I'm reachin' for my badge, Jordan," Hatfield said in a low voice. From its secret pocket he extracted the silver star on silver circle, emblem of the Texas Rangers and a sign to conjure with. "We had yore complaint and I come in answer to it."

"*Bueno,*" said Moss Jordan. "Glad yuh're here, Ranger. But it looks like it would take more than one officer to settle the hash of Dowie Burke and his gang."

Studying Moss Jordan, the Ranger decided that the former confederate colonel was over fifty. He was wiry and of medium height. Bushy, graying brows joined over alert gray eyes, and he had a sharp face and a peppery manner. He was now wearing dark pants and shirt.

"I like to work on the q.t. till I see what's what, Jordan," explained the Ranger.

"Yuh can trust those three," said Jordan, nodding toward the men who had withdrawn to one side. "Rob and Hank are my own men and the big hombre is Ben Naler, as square a young galoot as yuh'll ever meet. He's from across the Pecos and a visitor, but he's stayed to help in this fight. Burke and his gunslingers, I'm convinced, killed an old friend of mine named Styles. This is the second time they've tried for us, not countin' once when we found Styles' corpse in the monte and they chased us home. They were here last week but Naler was on guard and we beat 'em off."

"Let's see what we got over here," suggested Hatfield.

Jordan picked up the lantern and they went over to the silent figure lying near the dark woods. Hatfield rolled the body over. The Ranger slug had caught the killer in the back of the skull.

"I seen him over at Styles'," offered Moss Jordan. "He's

one of Burke's crew. They took over at Styles' after killin' Lon but when we found the body and complained to the county sheriff they hid out in the Yellow Hills. Sheriff come over and smelled around but after a couple of days huntin' he gave up and went off on another call. He ain't too sympathetic with me anyway. I fought under Stonewall Jackson and Jeb Stuart, yuh see, and the sheriff was put in by the carpetbaggers two years ago."

"I savvy."

Rob, Hank and Ben Naler joined them and stood around staring at the dead man. The light showed Naler as stalwart, and nearly as tall as the Ranger, a cowman by all signs. Hatfield liked Naler's looks, the bronzed young face and clear eyes. He liked the soft way Naler had of talking when he was not on the prod. He could speak out when need be, but otherwise saved his breath. The coppery hair on his well-shaped head was curly, and his eyes looked at a man squarely. He appeared to be quick with a pistol and all in all a valuable friend to have around.

Hank was young and smiling. Rob was older and silent, and a tobacco cud thrust out one leathery cheek.

"I'll get a shovel, boss," suggested Hank, "and we'll bury this lobo where he lies."

Jordan nodded, turning back with Hatfield.

"I'll tell yuh all we savvy," said the colonel. "But first let's go inside and have a drink. If yuh're hungry, Ranger, my daughter will shake yuh up a meal."

"I could do with a drink but I ate in town, thanks just the same."

Jordan carried the lantern as they went back toward the house. They passed close to the rock where Hatfield had had his match with Dowie Burke and the circle of yellow light showed the dark piece of shirt which Hatfield had ripped from Burke.

"Wait a jiffy, Jordan," said the Ranger, turning. "Fetch the light closer."

He stooped and picked up the sweated cloth. The flap of the breast pocket was open as the button had been pulled from its moorings, and Hatfield glimpsed edges of a sheet of white paper sticking out. He drew it forth and unfolded it, holding it to the lantern so he could see what it was.

Moss Jordan looked over his shoulder as he bent to read the words inscribed on the paper. There were several names on it, headed by that of Lon Styles. A line had been drawn through Styles' name. The second on the list was that of Moss Jordan.

"Yuh savvy who all these folks are?" inquired Hatfield, his gray-green eyes gleaming as he looked around at Jordan.

"Shore. Styles is dead. I'm next. The third is John Phelps, a neighbor across the river. He's got a farm runnin' back from the valley. Lives there with his wife and four kids. The fourth is Sam Olliphant, up the line from me. He's owner of a small ranch." Moss Jordan knew the people on the list. "They're all decent folks, Hatfield, and they all live within fifteen miles of here in the Yellow Hills. That last one scrawled in different writin' is Ben Naler."

"Huh," observed the Ranger. "Looks like Naler's name was added after the list was complete."

The handwriting was round and even, each letter formed with scrupulous care, except for Naler's which had been inscribed by someone not used to holding a pen or pencil.

They went on to the house as the Ranger pocketed the strange list. He was taking a graver and graver view of it as he turned it over in his mind. Styles was already dead. They had tried for Moss Jordan.

A girl standing in front of the porch hurried to Jordan and Naler.

"What was it?" she asked. "Burke again?"

"Yes, Connie," answered Jordan. "They've gone now. We're safe."

Moss Jordan led the way inside and struck a match. It had been Jordan who had been between the lamp and window and the bullet sent by Burke had missed by two feet, smashing the pane of glass and going high, thanks to Hatfield's action. Jordan lighted the table lamp and turned to the tall officer who bulked in the front door. Naler and the girl stood facing Hatfield.

"My daughter Connie," said Jordan. "Meet Mr. Hatfield, Connie."

The Ranger swept his Stetson off and bowed gallantly. Connie Jordan was exquisite. The plain blue calico dress she wore could not hide the loveliness of her figure, and such golden hair and liquid amber eyes as hers would cast a spell over any man. Hatfield was no exception and his glance was frankly admiring.

She smiled at him. "I'll fetch something to drink," she said, and went toward the back of the house.

Hatfield followed her with his eyes. Then he looked back and caught Ben Naler's gaze. He was startled at the scowl on the young cowman's pleasant face. But as he realized why, he felt amused. Naler was jealous.

But the Ranger had vital things on his mind. The death list burned in his pocket. Speed of action would mean life to the proscribed men on it. He could not rest till they were warned.

Connie came back carrying a tray with a pitcher of cider and a plate of sugared doughnuts on it. There was whisky in the bottle on the sideboard.

The Ranger sat down at the table with Jordan. Naler shook his head and took a chair in the corner. The young fellow looked sulky as Connie busied herself waiting on the visitor and her father.

Hatfield knew what was the matter with Naler and studiously avoided any further exchanges with the pretty girl. When Connie went out into the kitchen again, Ben Naler got up and followed her.

Rob and Hank were outside, burying the dead outlaw. One of them would stay on guard through the night.

"Yuh're right to keep a sentry out, Jordan," Hatfield said. "I'm thinkin' we oughtn't to waste any time in warnin' yore friends and neighbors on this list we snatched from Dowie Burke. In my opinion every man on it will be killed."

Moss Jordan jumped and his thick brows drew together.

"By Jupe yuh're right, Ranger! Come to think of it that list has to mean what yuh say. They aim to clean out the Yellow Hills!"

"Why?" asked Hatfield.

Moss Jordan shrugged. "Yuh got me there. I been wonderin' why they'd bother to kill a harmless old fossil like Lon and an old coot like me. Styles' place ain't worth fifty cents an acre. I got a few blooded hosses but they ain't tried to steal 'em."

Hatfield thought it over but as yet he could not guess the reason for Burke's attack on the inhabitants of the Yellow Hills.

The cool cider had a piquant tang and went down easily. He was dry from the powerful exertions against the drygulchers. He tried a doughnut and it was delicious, the crust crisp and the inside soft and tasty. Before the big officer knew it he had nearly emptied the platter.

"Yore daughter make 'em?" he asked.

"Yes, suh. She's a mighty good cook."

Naler trailed Connie back into the front room. Hatfield rose. He did not want to worry Naler, for he wanted the young cowman to be an ally and friend. Naler might have a sense of humor, but he was in deadly earnest over the girl.

"I'm in favor of gettin' those warnin's out tonight, Jordan," said the Ranger grimly. "When I was on my way here I saw Dowie Burke and his men crossin' the river a few miles back toward Stuart's Ford. S'pose they returned that way? Whose place would it bring 'em closest to?"

"Jack Phelps' farm," replied Jordan.

"Burke would be mighty riled at what happened. That sort of turkey is apt to lash out blind and take out his rage on whoever is near. He's lost his list but he'd likely remember some of the names on it, Phelps comes after yores."

Moss Jordan agreed. "I don't dare leave Connie here unguarded, though," he objected.

"Tell me how to reach Phelps' and I'll go there myself," said the Ranger. "Send Rob and Hank with notes to warn the others. You stick here with Naler and watch yore home."

CHAPTER VI

Men of the Yellow Hills

Naler, Hatfield knew, was not acquainted with the Yellow Hills, but neither was the Ranger. Hatfield was sure, though, that he could find the Phelps farm in the night if given explicit directions. Anyhow, he preferred to leave Naler with Jordan for there was always a chance that Burke might double back and again try to kill Moss.

Jordan gave him a brief note to John Phelps. Hatfield would pose for a time as simply a friend of Jordan's, until he could see what was what in the district.

The Ranger left Jordan busy writing further warnings to the people of the Yellow Hills. He whistled, and after a short time the golden sorrel came to him. Mounting,

Hatfield started back on the road. When he had made a few miles he turned and crossed the stream.

He was alert and ready for anything, but only the moon-bathed hills loomed before him as he climbed from the valley. Save for the sounds of nature the land seemed peaceful and deserted.

After about an hour's ride from the Colorado crossing he sighted the lights of a house, set back from the river.

"That will be it, Goldy," he murmured.

He dismounted out from the circle of light and scouted closer. He could see no horses and as he strained his ears to listen he caught the sound of a woman in the house sobbing, sobbing with heart-broken violence.

Hatfield knew then what must have happened. He knocked at the front door and the crying checked. There was a silence and then a frightened voice gasped:

"Who is it?"

"I'm a friend, ma'am," replied the Ranger gently. "Moss Jordan sent me to warn yuh. But I reckon I'm too late."

After a time the bolt was pulled back and the door opened. The tall officer looked down on a small woman with black hair drawn tightly back from her pallid face. Her eyes were red from weeping and when Hatfield glanced past her he saw a man lying on the couch.

It was difficult for her to speak.

"My husband," she whispered. "Dead!" She was evidently suffering from shock.

"Mama!" a child called. "Who's there?"

"It's all right, Johnny," she soothed, trying to keep the anguish and fright from her voice as she reassured the boy.

Fury burned the tall Ranger. Seeing the stricken family who had lost husband and father made him grind his teeth in baffled anger. Beaten off at Jordan's, the vicious Dowie Burke and his bunch had struck Phelps and killed. . . .

The next morning broke bright and warm over the Yellow Hills. Mrs. Phelps had refused to leave her husband's body during the night but she had promised that she would come with her children to Jordan's after the burial, which would take place that day.

Hatfield had ridden back to Jordan's. Rob and Hank, he found, had been out till dawn spreading the warning to the men involved. A few hours' sleep had restored Hatfield and given Goldy a chance to rest. By the time the Ranger was in the kitchen, eating a hearty breakfast of hot cakes and bacon, washed down by several cups of coffee and set before the men by Connie, Moss Jordan, meantime, had despatched Rob to Phelps' with a wagon to bring Mrs. Phelps and the children back. Rob would pitch in and help the widow and her sister straighten things up. By that time other neighbors would be on hand and Connie and Moss intended to ride over for the burial later in the day.

Ben Naler trailed Hatfield out into the stable yard. They rolled smokes and lighted up, Naler politely holding a match for the Ranger. Moss Jordan was working around the stables.

"That Dowie Burke is a mad dog and ought to be shot on sight," observed Naler.

Hatfield nodded. "I'd like to get hold of him, Naler."

Naler was a naturally friendly young fellow. But he was head over heels in love with Connie Jordan and as yet had not dared test his luck by asking her to marry him, and he also could see that the tall stranger impressed men and women with his power and manner. So the green-eyed monster had eaten at his soul.

But since the Ranger had noted how Naler felt, he had taken care not to show too much interest in the pretty girl. And of course Naler could have no idea who Hatfield was, since the Ranger had told only Moss Jordan of his real identity. Now both men were doing their best to keep a friendly spirit uppermost.

41

The sun was coming up and the world was lovely. Nearby ran the river and the Yellow Hills rose about them. The valley road, which had been such a danger spot in the night, was empty and stretched along in a winding yellow ribbon. In the blue sky here and there could be seen stains of smoke where some farm or other settler's home stood.

"They got some nice hosses here," offered Naler.

The top halves of the doors in the stalls stood open and a dozen horses had their heads out. Naler led the Ranger down the line, introducing him to each horse. Here it was a matter of quality rather than quantity.

The animals were beautifully groomed and cared for and as spoiled as petted children. They were far different horses than the chunky wild mustangs of the Plains. Their legs were slender and they were taller, with arched necks and the mettled nerves of pedigreed creatures. Three of the mares had colts with them.

"I shore love hosses," said Ben Naler, fondling the silky neck of a chestnut mare who nuzzled at him.

"Me too." Hatfield nodded. "A good one is the best friend a man could have."

"My idea is to buy some good stock and try to improve the breed on my ranch out there," continued Naler. "Jordan has the best I've seen. He's mighty careful and good at breedin' 'em. If he had a little money he could do a mighty fine job but he lost his last peso in the war."

Jordan, Naler explained, had brought a few animals from Kentucky. They were Arabian strain. But it was slow business, building up any backlog of stock to sell.

Naler and Hatfield pitched in to assist Jordan with the chores. Hank was sleeping somewhere in the barn as he had been up all night carrying warnings to the neighbors. After rubbing down and petting each horse the animals were turned into a grassy pasture fenced along the river. The colts kicked up their long legs and frolicked around their mothers as they made the circuit of the pen in their morning constitutional.

By the time the men had finished and had washed up, Connie had tidied the house and was dressing to go to the Phelps home. Moss Jordan saddled his own and his daughter's riding horses. Hatfield made Goldy ready and Naler had a rangy bay gelding to ride.

Jordan's shrewd horseman's eyes examined Goldy. He walked around the sorrel a couple of times and pushed back his hat, his eyes narrowing.

"He's a beaut," said Jordan. "Even if I was tryin' to buy him I couldn't find anything wrong."

The four reached the Phelps place after noon. The preacher had been sent for from town and neighbors had come in wagons or on horseback for the funeral. Mrs. Phelps had regained some of her composure, although she was pale and nervous. The children were young, ranging from three years old to nine—two boys and two girls.

The women had pitched in and taken over. The house had been set aright and all was ready.

Everybody knew Moss Jordan, and the colonel introduced Naler and Hatfield. The Ranger met Sam Olliphant, who owned a little ranch up the river from Jordan's. Olliphant, a big, breezy man of forty in clean range clothing, had a wife and children and hired five cowboys.

Van Lewis was another whose name was on the death list now in the Ranger's pocket. Lewis was a former Confederate soldier and owned a farm north of Phelps' in the Yellow Hills. He was short and slim, dark of features, a silent man with expressive black eyes.

Mark Ellsworth, still another of Dowie Burke's intended victims, had a cabin down the river just above Stuart's Ford. He had a small income, raised crops in season, and had a few cows and chickens to eke out a

43

living for his growing family. He was under thirty and was clad in "Sunday" clothes for the funeral.

The names on the list resolved thus into living people with the hopes and fears of humanity, men on whom women and children depended for life itself. Hatfield gauged them and liked them. They had faults and foibles, but so did all men.

The Ranger shook hands with stout "Pop" Murphy, whose Irish brogue was amusing to hear and whose good nature never deserted him.

"Pop's the champion of the hills," Moss Jordan explained, grinning. "He's got more kids than anybody else. How many is it, Pop—fourteen or fifteen?"

"Ah I lose count of the rascals meself." Murphy grinned too.

Murphy had had a warning from Jordan, for his name was on the death paper. Now he questioned Moss about it, seeking to understand what was going on.

"We ain't shore," replied Jordan. "But we figger that Dowie Burke and his gunslingers aim to clean us all out of the Yellow Hills. They got Phelps and they got Styles. They tried for me a couple times."

"Then we should band together and run this Burke devil into the Gulf," declared Murphy. "In union there is strength, say I."

"Yuh're right there, Murphy," agreed Hatfield. "It's a mighty good idea. S'pose we tip off yore friends concerned, Jordan, while they're all together today?"

That suited Moss Jordan.

All the men were curious about the grim warning sent them by Jordan, as was natural. Duke Ulman, a rancher, Charlie Sutton, a farmer, and four more men were on the list and Hatfield and Jordan talked with all of them while waiting for the services to begin. . . .

Later in the afternoon, when the remains of John Phelps had been given proper burial, Hatfield collected a dozen riders and, led by Jordan and Naler, they made the run to Lon Styles' shack in the hills, where Dowie Burke had been seen.

But the cabin was deserted. Burke and his men were not around. But there was sign of them, when Hatfield and Ben Naler checked up around the place.

"They were here not long ago, mebbe this mornin' early," said the Ranger. "Wish I could get one good look at that killer—over my sights."

As yet the tall officer had not had a good look at Burke, for he had not seen the man in the daylight. His contact with the leader of the killers had been confined to the events of the night when he had clashed with Dowie in the darkness.

The men of the Yellow Hills had been keyed up for a real fight with Dowie Burke and now they felt let down, with the birds flown. They had gone on a wild-goose chase, and were subdued as they returned to the Phelps ranchhouse.

The people there were making ready to return to their homes. Mrs. Phelps and her family would go to Jordan's although they had a dozen offers of hospitality. Rob had had a nap and would drive the wagon with the guests in it. Connie and Moss Jordan on their horses, and several neighbors going across the river and up the valley road would accompany them as far as Jordan's farm.

"Naler, you've seen Dowie Burke," said Hatfield. "From the trail they left they may have headed to Stuart's Ford. Mebbe we could spot Burke if we went there. Are yuh game?"

"Shore I'm game. Wait till I tell Connie and Colonel Jordan."

As the two young men set off toward the town the sun was behind them and growing red, preparing to drop behind the Yellow Hills.

CHAPTER VII

Stuart's Ford

Light of day was gone when Hatfield and Ben Naler sighted the settlement, and it was growing darker as they rode down Main Street. Lamps had come on and the Palace—the hotel and largest saloon—was brightly lighted. The smell of supper cooking was in the warm air. Men and women were about, and horses and teams stood in the gutters.

Naler and Hatfield pulled up near the Palace.

"There's Dowie Burke now, goin' into the saloon!" Naler said suddenly. "See him? That big hound in the leather jacket and brown Stetson? Two of his men with him."

"Keep back," warned the Ranger. "Let 'em get inside."

In the shadows of the long wooden awning over the sidewalk they quietly dismounted.

"I'll make the play, Naler," said Hatfield.

Naler looked around at him. "Burke's mighty tough."

Naler was curious about Hatfield, wondering how he had happened to come to the Yellow Hills. The Ranger understood that. He knew that Naler had an inquisitive, perhaps suspicious mind but a man needed one to survive in the country where Naler lived. A man could not trust every rider who came along.

It was not etiquette to ask questions as to a man's past, but a stranger needed to prove himself to the hilt with such a person as Naler. Motives were uppermost in Naler's brain. Hatfield already had done his best to stop Naler worrying about Connie, but now he knew that to ensure Naler's wholehearted cooperation he must tell the young cowman just who and what he was.

He touched the tall young rancher's shoulder.

"I come here in answer to Jordan's call for help, Naler," he said in a low voice. "I'm a Texas Ranger, Jim Hatfield's my real handle. I like to work quietlike till I see what's what, savvy? So keep it to yoreself. If anybody asks yuh just say I'm yore pardner out on yore ranch."

The confidence pleased Naler and flattered him.

"A Ranger! I thought yuh were a mighty salty passerby! I'm with yuh all the way, Hatfield. Shake!"

His grip was firm and the invisible wall which Naler had kept between himself and Hatfield melted away. He had become a wholehearted ally instead of a questioning one.

The Palace had a second floor and up front was a balcony with lighted windows open on it.

"Somebody's in the A suite," remarked Naler, who had stayed at the Palace before stopping at Jordan's, and knew how the settlement hotel aped city caravansaries in numbering its rooms.

"I'll go in first and turn to the bar on the right," said Hatfield. "You follow me, Naler. Don't make any play unless Burke forces it or I open the ball."

"Right."

Hatfield ducked under the rail and stepped up on the wide porch. The batwings were open and he could look down the long bar. Sawdust was on the floor and there were tables and benches on his left, the bar on his right. It was lively, with plenty of thirsty customers at this time of day.

The two riders who had entered with Dowie Burke were halfway down the line and had shouldered to the counter. They were banging with their fists and calling for drinks. But the Ranger could not see Burke.

Naler sauntered in and turned to the bar without looking at the tall Ranger, who stood against the front wall. Naler was seen by Burke's men and they began to scowl as they assumed a ready attitude. Both wore two Colts, and they were bearded, dirty and tough in aspect. They dog-eyed the imperturbable Naler who feigned not to notice.

A closed door was at the back of the saloon. Over on the far side of the tables was an open archway leading into a long hall with a counter and desk. Behind this desk sat a middle-aged woman, the proprietor's wife. A wooden staircase led to the floor above and on the counter was a large ledger used as a hotel register. Hatfield had signed it when he had hired a bed for a sleep at the time of his arrival in Stuart's Ford.

Hatfield saw a small hole in the crowd up front and moved to the bar. Naler stood behind a cowboy, waiting his turn.

The Ranger was halfway through his slow drink before Dowie Burke came down the stairs and crossed the lobby, pausing in the archway to sweep the saloon with a swift gaze. Naler cleared his throat and coughed loudly. Burke frowned as he recognized Naler but did not make any threatening move. Instead Dowie turned and went to the rear of the saloon.

In the bright light Burke was a tough-looking proposition. Hatfield could understand why he had had such a tussle with the man. Burke must weigh over two hundred but he was not fat at all. He had a massive fighting jaw and hot black eyes. His curly black hair was long around his ears and down the nape of his bulldog neck.

There were bruises and fresh scratches on his sullen face, no doubt marks of the wrestling match with the Ranger. When Burke raised a hand to signal the bar-keeper it looked as though he were waving a cured ham. He had on a leather jacket and old chaps, Stetson, half-boots and blue pants. Crossed belts at his burly waist supported his well-kept guns.

"That hand of Burke's never wrote them fine letters on my list," mused Hatfield. "If he can scrawl he's lucky."

Had someone given Burke the death roster so that Dowie would know whom to kill in the Yellow Hills?

Hatfield could see through the wide archway into the lobby. Now another man came downstairs but he was entirely different from Burke in appearance. He was an elegant personage—that could be told at a glance. His portly figure was clad in a fine dark suit, with a white shirt and stock at his bearded throat. The light glinted on highly polished shoes of the softest leather. In the stock rode a big solitaire diamond darting rainbow colors as it caught the lamplight, and there were jewels in the rings on his well-kept white hands. He carried a thick cane and the cut of his coat permitted much of his fancy vest to be seen, with a massive gold chain and diamond fob suspended from pocket to pocket.

Hatfield took in the eagle look of the elegant one's face with the strong nose and dominant eyes.

"He must have had that A suite," decided the Ranger. "Nothin' else would do! I wonder if he's the man Dowie Burke went upstairs to pow-wow with?"

The bearded swell swept the bar with his glance and though he stared straight at Dowie Burke no sign of recognition passed between them. Drawn by the puzzle of it all, the Ranger moved over closer, feigning to be hunting a seat at a table near the connecting passage.

The bearded man had reached the desk. His face seamed with a smile as he lifted his black hat to the woman there in a courtly gesture. In a strong, commanding voice he said:

"The fare was most excellent, Mrs. Rolls. I have seldom tasted better and I have eaten in many places and countries. *Experto credite,* as they say— Believe one who knows by experience!"

"Thank you, sir," she said with a smile. "Come again."

The gentleman paid his bill from a large roll and carelessly shoved the remainder back in a pocket. A slim, dark-faced Spanish-looking man in a plain black suit and derby hat came down, carrying two heavy bags. The swell at the desk raised his hat in farewell to the proprietress and went outside, the man with the valises following.

Hatfield could see the hotel's exit, another door from that of the bar. The stout man was helped into a shining buggy drawn by two fast grays. The thin servant treated his master with the most obsequious attention, arranging a carriage robe over his knees and holding a match to the cigar clenched between the bearded lips.

Hatfield slipped outside. The windows of the A suite were dark, the lamps having been blown out by those leaving. The Spanish servitor was stowing the valises in the back compartment of the buggy. He closed the top and climbed to the driver's seat, taking the reins and clucking to the grays. They moved off in a rush. The wheels were greased and the patent-leather body creaked as the carriage drew away and disappeared on the east road from Stuart's Ford.

The Ranger rubbed his chin thoughtfully. He was definitely interested. He went through the door on the hotel side and touched his Stetson to the woman who gave him an earnest look and then a smile.

"That's quite a gent who just left, ma'am," he observed off-handedly.

"That's Mr. Tynsdale," she informed him.

"He been here before?"

"Oh yes. This is his fourth visit."

The register lay open. Stuart's Ford had few visitors from the outside world. Hatfield read the names. His own signature was there and so was Naler's. The last guest to sign had been the elegant swell who had just left in the buggy. The Ranger stared at the line:

Sidney Tynsdale, Esq., Houston Tex.

Coldness prickled up and down the tall officer's spine. The handwriting was round and even, each letter scrupulously formed, showing the determined character of the author and his intense application to details. Hatfield was certain that he had seen a specimen of that writing before—on the death roster in his pocket!

The discovery opened a mystifying and alarming vista to the Ranger. Burke had loomed large, but from the facts Hatfield could now deduce Dowie was only an agent, a tool of a much cleverer, more dangerous man.

The latest Tynsdale signature was on the right hand side of the ledger. Hatfield's quick eye traveled up the lines and on the other page he found Tynsdale again. The date was a day before that of Lon Styles' killing.

"Mind if I turn back a few pages, ma'am?" he begged softly, looking the woman in the eye. "I was hopin' to find an old pard in these parts."

"Go ahead, sir," she replied. "Help yourself." He had a deep respect and courtesy for women and none could look upon the tall Ranger without realizing that.

Tynsdale, he found, had been in Stuart's Ford on four occasions, as the woman had said. At least he had registered at the hotel that many times. The first visit to the vicinity recorded in the hotel register had been about a month previously.

"Must be a mighty urgent reason to draw such an hombre to a neck in the woods like this!" Hatfield thought.

He turned over his information in his alert mind.

"I'll bet Tynsdale wrote that list and gave it to Dowie Burke," he decided. "Then Dowie added Ben Naler's name. If it ain't so I'll eat my hat, strap, runner and all."

None of his excitement, however, showed in his rugged, bronzed face which the proprietress regarded with admiration. Her voice startled him from his reverie.

"Do you ever write to your mother?" she inquired.

"You ought to, you know. She would worry about you. Here's an envelope and paper and pen. I'll mail it for you."

"You're mighty sweet, ma'am," he murmured. "But my mother's dead."

Sympathy touched her eyes. She sighed. Added to the big young man's other attractions was the fact he was an orphan.

"Who was the Spanish lookin' hombre with Tynsdale?" he asked.

"That's Felipe Palacio, Mr. Tynsdale's secretary and aide."

Suddenly Hatfield whirled on the balls of his feet, for a difference in the sounds from the noisy saloon warned him of danger. It was an abrupt menace and Hatfield realized what it was as he looked through the archway and saw a tough confronting Ben Naler.

His trained eye told the Ranger instantly they were after Naler and meant to kill! Hatfield's glance flicked to Dowie Burke to see just where the burly chief stood. Dowie was still down the bar and close to his two men. Burke and everybody else for that matter were staring at Naler and the plug-ugly challenging the rancher!

CHAPTER VIII

A Narrow Squeak

Although there had seemed to be no room at the bar a few moments ago there was plenty of space cleared now, as men sought to get out of the line of fire. Experts at judging the paths flying lead might take, spectators silently set themselves. Naler had turned with his back to the mirror and rail. He had one high heel hooked in the footrest and his elbows on the edge of the bar. A wide-bodied man in a black shirt and scratched riding leather, and with a dark Stetson curved over his low brow, was cursing Naler. Hatfield could see the deep red of the bull neck and glimpse a dirty cheek with beard stubble on it.

"Yuh stepped on my foot, cuss yuh!" snarled the tough. "Ain't there enough room in the world without a two-bit nogood hound like you havin' to walk all over yore betters?" He ended with virulent abuse and paused for breath.

Naler's clear drawl reached everybody in the saloon.

"Run along, sonny, or I'll wash out yore mouth with soap for usin' such language."

Ridicule was one thing that such a gunslinger's ego could not brook and the titter from the listeners goaded Burke's man to blind fury. With a hoarse shout he threw a punch at Naler but the rancher weaved his head aside. Raising a spurred foot and heaving up on the rail, braced against the bar, Naler drove a kick into the tough's middle and sent him sprawling in the sawdust.

Hatfield had reached the archway now—just in time to see the gunslinger come to his knees and whip out a Colt, the weapon rising and cocking under his blunt thumb as he pointed at Naler for the kill.

Three pistols seemed to explode simultaneously. Naler and Hatfield had both drawn and fired and the tough's gun went off, too. Hatfield saw Naler jump. The rancher stood before the bar and stared as Dowie Burke's killer dropped his arm and fell on his face, wriggling in the wet sawdust.

But the Ranger dared not waste an instant of time, for he knew Dowie Burke was the dangerous one. Burke was after Naler and had sent the gunhand to draw out the rancher.

Hatfield whirled around. The woman at the desk had screamed once and then ducked behind the counter.

"Outside—run for it, Naler!" shouted the Ranger even as he hurried a shot off to take care of Burke.

Down the bar Dowie Burke had made a draw and even now was about to kill Naler. His two companions had their Colts out and rising, to blast the cowman. Hatfield tried for Burke with a snap shot, as the crowd surged back. He did not wish to injure any innocent bystanders, but as he raised his thumb off his pistol hammer one of Dowie's followers darted between the Ranger's position and Burke and caught the heavy slug in the shoulder.

Guns were snapping but Burke's aim was wrecked as his own man blundered against him, howling with pain and clutching his right arm. The other gunslinger was blocked and shoved aside by the retreating customers.

Ben Naler had jumped for the door as Hatfield sharply warned him. Burke was behind some others and aware of the Ranger's fire. He sent a quickie which knocked a long splinter from the side of the archway. Hatfield drew back, but Naler was given another few moments to make the exit as Hatfield attracted Burke's lead.

Nobody wanted to be near the participants and Burke had to shift as he found himself in the open with his tall opponent partly sheltered by the wall. With a sharp cry Burke slid over the bar and dropped behind it. The barkeepers had already ducked. Both of Dowie's men dashed for the back door.

Hatfield sent a couple across the bar at the point where Dowie Burke had disappeared. It delayed Dowie's bobbing up to shoot again and when the burly killer showed a few feet from the spot where he had disappeared behind the bar, Ben Naler was outside.

Burke began hooting and whistling as Hatfield's tearing lead forced his head down. There was a brief lull in the fire and gray gunsmoke drifted to the heated areas around the hanging gilt oil lamps.

Crouched at the edge of the archway Hatfield heard answering howls to Burke's calls. More of Dowie's followers must be close at hand and were coming.

The Ranger turned and pelted out through the hotel exit. He bumped violently into Ben Naler who was coming back inside to help him in the fight.

"Watch it!" gasped Naler. "Six or eight of Burke's boys are runnin' up the street."

A stentorian challenge came from the plaza. A lone man came galloping toward the Palace.

"Halt there! Cut it out!"

"That's the marshal," said Naler hurriedly.

The lone constable was brave enough as he charged toward the center of the disturbance. Dowie Burke had thrown open a side window and was calling his men by name as he urged them into the fray. Burke was hard, and as far as physical prowess went he was a dangerous opponent.

Naler was limping.

"Is it bad?" asked Hatfield.

"No, just a burn. That first one cut my boot wide open."

"We better sashay. No sense in makin' a fight here. They outnumber us and they'll shoot us in the back if they get the chance. Come on!"

Hatfield and Naler trotted across the wooden walk to duck under the hitch-rail. Goldy and Naler's horse were up the way and the two men hit leather and turned along Main. Dowie Burke plummeted from the dark slit between the Palace and the next building. He had come out the side window and was calling up his crowd in a brassy voice.

"There they go! They downed Nifty! Kill 'em! It's Naler and a pard of his!"

The main gang had come up now and they all began

sending shots after the Ranger and Naler. But they had only a few brief glimpses of the fleeing pair as they crossed the creek, drawing out of easy Colt range.

Dowie Burke's fighting dander was up, though, and he did not mean to give up so easily. He called to his followers who picked up their mustangs and set out after the two who had come out ahead in the brief encounter at the Palace. Blood lust burned in Burke's hard soul.

The moon was up. The creek road quickly petered out into the main dirt road running along the south bank of the river. Hatfield and Naler passed another wooden bridge and stayed on that side, the rising hills showing black against the silver sky. Dust swirled from the beating hoofs.

Hatfield glanced back over a hunched shoulder.

"Here they come!" he remarked.

They had a few hundred yards start. Dowie Burke and perhaps ten more riders were bunched together and were silhouetted against the lighted settlement as they flogged and spurred their horses.

Since his discovery of Sidney Tynsdale, the Ranger had lost much of his interest in Dowie Burke. Contempt entered into his account of Burke, contempt for a slow-witted killer who showed his hand and was marked for the law and for vengeance. Burke was an outlaw and no doubt a proficient gunfighter in a knockdown-dragout fight. But he had no finesse.

Sidney Tynsdale loomed large in the Ranger's imagination. Because of Burke's stupidity Hatfield had been set on Tynsdale's trail. He would never leave it now until either he or Tynsdale was done for.

"They're pickin' up!" called Naler. "We better hustle."

"Lead 'em on and tire out their hosses for a while," said Hatfield. He swung in the saddle to fire a long one back at the pursuers. They replied with howls and a burst of Colts, but the range was too far and the jolting pace ruined any attempt at accurate aim.

After a half-hour of teasing the ravening enemy, Hatfield said:

"Come on, let's hit the ford just above here, Naler!"

"All right. But it takes us away from Jordan's. Ain't we headin' there?"

"Not me. Not yet, anyway. I got an idea."

"They're usually good ones," said Naler, the words jolted from him by the motion of the big horse under him. "Let's have it."

"We'll keep Burke on our trail as long as we can. It will tire their hosses. They'll hunt a place to rest and if we're near Styles' shack they may go there for a while. Savvy?"

Naler rode on for fifty yards, then said:

"I guess I do. While they're holed up at Styles', one of us can fetch Jordan and enough fightin' men to wipe out Burke and his bunch."

"Yuh get a gold star for that," the Ranger applauded.

He cut down across a meadow and with Naler near him crossed the Colorado. They rode up the opposite slant for a hundred yards and Hatfield sent a couple of betraying shots at Burke.

The still furious gunslinger yelped and shot replies. They came swarming across the river and up the slope on Hatfield's trail. The riding grew rough as there was no road along the route the Ranger picked. But he must tire out the mustangs. Goldy and Naler's rangy bay were better horses and could last longer.

For two hours the Ranger managed to draw Burke and his killers on into the Yellow Hills.

But at last the pursuers gave up. Hatfield and Naler stopped and turned to shoot at Burke and his bunch but they could not make them come any further.

"They're through," said Hatfield. "Come on, let's go over the hill."

Naler and the Ranger moved slowly to a wooded slope. In the trees Hatfield turned and watched. They

57

could see the dark figures of their enemies in the hollow. Cigarettes glowed red as the gunslingers lighted up and let their horses blow.

After a time Burke led his men north.

"They're headin' for the trail up there," said Naler.

"I reckon that leads to Styles' eventually," said Hatfield.

"That's right."

At a safe distance they shadowed Burke and his riders. From a height overlooking the north bank road they saw and heard the bunch go by, headed in the direction of Lon Styles' cabin. Carefully, trailing by the risen dust and by ear, Hatfield and Naler ended up near the little shack where Styles had lived and died. Creeping close, they could see the mustangs in the open space. On the outside hearth the killers were lighting a fire. They were hungry after the long run.

Hatfield and Naler drew off and the Ranger gave his orders in a low voice.

"You go warn Moss Jordan. Fetch as many fighters as yuh can. I'll meet yuh here. Make it as near dawn as possible—that's a good time to attack. We'll sweep up Burke and his men and try to make 'em talk. There's somethin' I want to smell out, beyond Burke."

"What's that?"

"I can't go into it right now. There ain't time. Get goin'."

Naler touched the Ranger's hand and led his horse down the rocky hillside to a point where he could mount and ride.

Hatfield rubbed the lather off the sorrel and eased the cinches. When he had rested a bit he left Goldy in the patch of woods and moved closer to the cabin. A small fire glowed in the hearth and he could scent coffee and frying beef as the outlaws fixed themselves a satisfying meal before turning in. Their figures showed against the red glow and he could pick out Dowie Burke and several others he had seen in Stuart's Ford.

There was open space around the cabin but the two hills it nestled between cast black shadows and there were many uneven hummocks and protruding rocks to offer cover. Burke evidently believed that he and his men were safe at the spot for the moment. They had been chasing Naler and the unknown man who had interfered to save the rancher, and it was not in Burke's mind that the rabbit would turn and pursue the hounds.

Hatfield moved around to the shadowed side and downwind. He could catch their gruff voices as they had begun to eat and drink from bottles they had with them. The Ranger took off his boots and gunbelt and smeared dirt on his face and hands to kill any sheen of flesh. He left his Stetson behind and began crawling carefully closer to his foes.

Adept at the art, he reached a point where he could overhear what they were talking about.

CHAPTER IX

The Black Forest

The men were lighting cigarettes after their meal while some busily spiked tin cups of steaming coffee from whisky flasks and squatted to drink. A couple of them were close to Dowie Burke's burly figure. Peering past the bulge of the cabin, Hatfield could see the vicious, big-jawed face of the leader as Burke's eyes glowed from the firelight.

"I tell yuh I don't like it, Dowie," a bearded outlaw was objecting.

"What's wrong?" growled Burke. "Yuh yellow?"

"No, and yuh savvy I ain't. This country is as safe right now as a hornet nest. They've spotted us and they'll come after us. What are we in this for—love or money? Yuh can't spend yore cash when yuh're buzzard bait."

There was a muttering of agreement. Burke's reply was rather mild. He was willing to discuss the matter with his followers.

"We got Styles and Phelps, ain't we? That's a good start. We near took Naler tonight but that's only for fun. I hate his hide. What right had he to horn in on this party?"

"And who was that big galoot who wrecked our fun at the Palace?" demanded the other outlaw. "I never seen him before. And I hope I never do again, if yuh want the truth. He's too salty."

"Some pard of Naler's, that's all," replied Dowie but there was no conviction in his voice.

He, too, had been impressed at the Palace. He rubbed his ear speculatively for he had heard the close shriek of Hatfield's lead more than once during the evening.

"They're all up on their hind legs, Dowie," an owlhoot insisted. "Long as we could work on the quiet and in the dark it was fine with me. But look what happened at Jordan's last time. They near got yuh and yuh know it. We lost another man there. We're bein' whittled down."

Such men fought for money. They liked to hold a real advantage, too. Ardor cooled in them when they were faced with stern opposition. Burke stood alone against quitting the Yellow Hills and his argument was weak, as though he knew his men were right.

"I ain't goin' to stick at this place, not long, Dowie," warned his lieutenant. "They've been here after us and they'll come again. S'pose they set a trap here tonight? We'd have walked right in."

"If we stick I want more pay," declared another outlaw.

"All right," agreed Dowie, throwing up his hands. "We'll move out and lie low for a while till things quiet down."

The bearded gunslinger rose. "I'm sleepin' in the monte tonight. They ain't goin' to creep up on yores truly."

Hatfield was irritated, for the outlaws were making ready to shift. Their horses had had a short rest and they had eaten. He snaked slowly back, taking advantage of the stir they raised as they stamped out the fire and packed their belongings.

Later he followed them at a distance as they rode deep into the Yellow Hills. They went into a big woods and he could not follow on Goldy for he had no way of telling how far they had gone. He left the sorrel and crept to the forest, listening. All was silent save for the night insects and the faroff baying of a hound pack.

This terrain was entirely unfamiliar to him. He moved carefully into the woods and nearly ran over two men who had just settled down in their blankets in a tiny clearing. He froze to the ground.

"I had a plenty," he heard one say. "I'm pullin' out."

Hatfield drew back bit by bit. He concluded that Burke's bunch had split up and had hidden themselves through the dense woods to sleep. He could do nothing more, and weariness clutched at him. He slid back to the sorrel and saw to his horse for the night. Then he hid himself and snatched a sleep. . . .

The gray of dawn woke him. He saddled up and went to the spot where he had agreed to meet Ben Naler and the men of the Yellow Hills. The sun was just reddening the sky when he saw Naler coming up the wooded, rocky slope with Moss Jordan. They had brought along a dozen fighters, among them Olliphant, Duke Ulman, Charlie Sutton and Murphy, all on Burke's death list.

"They've moved," the Ranger informed them as they gathered about him. "They're three miles on, over the

61

mountain. There's a big patch of pine woods where they holed up for the night."

"That must be what we call the Black Forest," said Moss Jordan. "It's a mighty big patch. We hunt through there in the fall."

"Come on, and we'll try to round 'em up," ordered the Ranger.

Burke's bearded aide had been right when he had said the Yellow Hills people were aroused. They were keyed up and in a shooting mood over the killings of Styles and Phelps and at the threat to their own lives. Hatfield glanced back as he rode up the mountain, glanced back at their grim faces and the steady way they gripped their guns. He would not need to urge those men to fight.

"I'd like to grab off a prisoner or two, boys," he said to Jordan and Naler. "There's somebody beyond Dowie Burke in this business."

It was broad daylight now and they could not hide their approach to the dense woods. Hatfield was out front. When he was a couple of hundred yards from the line of trees a warning shout went up and a gun banged. The bullet whirled over his head and he picked up speed as he charged.

There were aisles in the woods through which a horse could make a way. Jordan and his men were whooping it up as they followed the tall man on the sorrel. A few shots snarled at them from ahead. Through a long vista the Ranger had a quick glimpse of the startled Dowie Burke, looking back over his shoulder. Burke was mounted and with three of his men. Hatfield tried for him but Burke slid down a bank behind tall pine boles and out of sight.

Heavy firing hunted in the brush and leaves for the enemy. They could, when they paused to listen, hear Burke's bunch crashing through before them in full retreat. Occasionally an enemy slug whistled in the air or plugged into a tree.

"They're splittin' up," announced Hatfield, as he heard several separated parties up front.

All morning they pushed through the wilderness. The woods petered out finally in the northeast. Jordan and the other ranchers had come over fast and their horses had not been fresh when they had begun the chase, while Burke had had a night's rest.

They gave up after noon. They had lost sight entirely of Dowie Burke himself who had managed to elude them before the forest petered out. Far ahead they could see two outlaws slowly climbing a long slope as they beat a retreat.

The pursuers called it a day and gathered to rest themselves and their horses. Smokes were rolled and bottles brought forth. Most of them were jubilant, feeling triumphant.

"We shore chased them sidewinders out of the country!" chortled Murphy.

"They won't come back and if they do we'll be ready for 'em!" boasted Mark Ellsworth.

Moss Jordan seemed satisfied, too. "I believe we threw a real jolt into Burke," he declared.

Ben Naler was noncommittal. He watched his tall friend, Hatfield, on whose opinion he had come to count.

The Ranger shook his head. "Mebbe they won't come back and mebbe they will, boys," drawled Hatfield. "Yuh mustn't relax. Keep watch night and day. It means yore lives."

Moss Jordan's eyes narrowed. "What do yuh know?" he inquired at last.

"I'm not shore of anything yet," answered the Ranger. "But I believe there's more to this than Dowie Burke and his crowd. Has any man here ever heard tell of a dude by the handle of Sidney Tynsdale? I believe he's from Houston."

Blank looks were exchanged between the men of the Yellow Hills and heads slowly shook.

"Wait a jiffy!" spoke up Sam Olliphant. "One time I was huntin' a few of my cows in the hills. I run onto an hombre in black leather and he had a Spanish lookin' feller with him. I spoke to 'em, asked if they'd seen my cattle. They said no. I told my name and asked theirs and this swell with the beard says his was Tindale or somethin' like it. I didn't get it clear. The Spanish one stared at me without sayin' a word till it gave me the creeps. I was glad to be shut of 'em."

"How long ago was this?" asked Hatfield.

Olliphant considered. "I'd say a month or five weeks back."

Hatfield thought, "That must have been Tynsdale and Palacio scoutin' the hills. But why?" Aloud he said, "I aim to leave for a while and try to clear all this up so yuh'll be safe for shore. If Burke don't come back I figger more and worse killers may strike. So stick together and be on guard."

Moss Jordan asked all his neighbors to his horse farm for dinner that night. Hatfield wished to give Goldy a full rest and he needed the same tonic himself, so he returned to Jordan's. Ranchers supplied sides of beef and a whole pig was brought over. Home-made breads, cookies, pies, and preserves were contributed. Everybody brought something to eat and drink.

In deference to the widow of John Phelps there was no music and no undue celebrating. That evening the people gathered together and talked of their own problems and of the great world outside the little area they knew. They were homely folk for the most part and small landholders.

Most of them had been Confederate sympathizers and the older men had fought in the Southern armies. But the War had been over for some years and the children were growing up. They preferred peace and the regime of the carpetbaggers had been hard on all.

Hatfield ate a tremendous hot meal. He watched the

young men and especially Ben Naler, in whose suit he had grown interested for he had quickly come to like the rancher from the Pecos.

It was plain that Naler was not used to such gatherings, and he was modest and shy around women. He felt out of place and showed it. He made one or two attempts to draw closer to Connie Jordan. She had been extremely busy helping feed the large company but when she was able to relax she was surrounded by a knot of men, among them several young bachelors who paid their court to her.

Sleep tugged at Hatfield's eyelids after the heavy meal. He kept stifling yawns and finally he slipped out the back door and went to the haybarn where he turned in. . . .

At daybreak he was in the side corral saddling the golden sorrel. The damp mist from the river meadows rolled across the valley. He could hear Jordan's Kentucky thoroughbreds stamping in their stalls.

Naler came out and leaned on the rail watching him saddle up.

"Take me with yuh, Ranger?" asked Ben.

Hatfield thought it over. "Yuh really want to come?" he asked. "I might be able to use yuh. I've got to locate this Tynsdale in Houston and mebbe that's where Dowie Burke has run to."

Naler was eager to ride with him.

A number of guests had stayed for the night and some were stirring. Women were in the kitchen, building up the wood fire in the big iron stove.

Soon the appetizing odors of coffee and frying ham and eggs reached Hatfield and Naler.

Naler had saddled his rested bay gelding, a fine animal he had ridden over from his far-off home. They went inside and were fed by the women. Connie was in the kitchen.

"We're leavin' right after breakfast, ma'am," the Ranger told her. He watched the girl.

"You're going away, Ben?" she asked quietly.

"Yes'm."

She stopped smiling, then she nodded. "Good-by, Ben. Good-by, Jim."

Ben Naler looked crestfallen. He bit his lip and went out. There were half a dozen women bustling about the kitchen and they made him feel ill at ease.

Moss Jordan was up and noisily greeting the new day. "Rise and shine!" cried Jordan.

Blanketed figures in the rooms and on the porch began to stir.

CHAPTER X

Contact

Jim Hatfield and Ben Naler mounted and started for the road which led to Stuart's Ford and thence on to Houston. Naler rode with his chin on his chest. He was silent and his young face was grim.

Hatfield looked back at the house.

"She's standin' out in the yard to wave so-long, Naler," he murmured.

Ben Naler jumped in his saddle and glanced quickly around. When Connie saw that Naler was looking she waved, and the two men waved back. The morning breeze stirred her golden hair and the blue dress she wore under her white apron.

Around the bend they could no longer see her and Naler settled down again to his gloomy mood.

"She's mighty pretty," said the Ranger, without looking at Naler. "Plenty of young fellers would give their eye-teeth for a girl like her."

"I know that," said Naler, and there was agony in his voice.

"It's all right to be some jealous. Yuh can't help that and it's natural. But a woman sizes up a man in her own way just as a man does a girl, Ben. If she's ordinarily polite she'll smile and talk with friendly folks. On the other hand she makes up her mind secret-like and it often don't take her long to do it."

Naler rode on in his black mood, his face stony.

"Have yuh spoken to her yet?" inquired the Ranger softly.

Naler had a fierce pride and he scowled, but then he shrugged and did not take offense.

"No," he admitted, abashed. "I am afeared to, Jim. S'pose she says no?"

"I don't believe she will."

Naler perked up, but quickly grew depressed again.

"Yuh don't savvy. She takes care of Colonel Jordan and she can't leave him. I couldn't ask her to. She likes ranchin' and if Jordan would move near me that might be all right. I'd give him all the land he'd need. Still Jordan won't leave here, and I can't stick around forever. I got to get back to my ranch before rustlers steal all my stock. And there's a dozen young fellers in these parts who are courtin' Connie."

They picked up the pace, maintaining a brisk trot after the horses were warmed up. The sun was up ahead of them and the river flowed to their left as they moved along the valley road.

"Tell yuh what, Ben," said the Ranger finally. "I ain't got wings and a bow and arrer, but I'll play Cupid for yuh. I'll go and tell Jordan how things stand if yuh'll ask Connie when we get back from Houston."

"Yuh will?"

"Shore as it's hot where Burke and Tynsdale are goin'."

Naler drew in a deep breath of the warming air.

"I'm game. I'll do it!"

He seemed to feel more cheerful after this decision had been reached and the two young men began to chat and enjoy themselves as they moved along. . . .

Hatfield and Naler crossed the Colorado at Stuart's Ford. There was no sign of Burke and his men in the settlement. The Ranger and his saddle companion headed straight for Houston, leaving the valley of the Colorado behind them. In the afternoon they crossed the Brazos and rode through the flat Gulf plains.

They struck a dirt road and followed it past wide fields of cotton where Negro hands picked the crops and carried the laden baskets on their heads, singing as they labored. The wet wind from the mighty Gulf touched them, and the heat was like a steam bath.

It was still daylight when they sighted Houston ahead.

"It's an up and comin' town, Houston," remarked Hatfield. "Growin' like wildfire, Naler. San Jacinto battlefield is east-southeast of the city where old Sam Houston beat the head off Santa Ana."

"How far is Galveston?" asked Naler.

"Mebbe fifty miles southeast. That's Buffalo Bayou that Houston stands on. The town's a railroad and shippin' center, and more and more factories are comin' here."

Black smoke stained the sky from numerous brick chimney stacks. Naler sniffed at the tainted air. "I wouldn't like it," he said at once. "Hate cities."

"Me, too," Hatfield said, and added musingly, "Cotton, sugar, rice, lumber—why, Houston handles it alll Yuh need to watch her dust. I'll bet she outstrips every city in Texas for her size, and she's only been goin' forty years or so. Sam Houston himself helped lay the city out. I seen his house last time I was here, in Caroline Street. She was the capital of the Republic, yuh savvy, in the early days, before they moved to Austin."

It was Naler's first visit to the metropolis which was growing with mushroom speed. The sea touched the cotton fields and the nearby range. Commerce and all sorts of trade flourished in Houston and to it flocked variegated characters all bent on the same purpose, the making of money.

Here swarmed capitalists and workers, sailors resting after long voyages, ranchers and cowboys who had driven herds to market. There were storekeepers and other tradesmen serving the inhabitants, the half world of gamblers and painted women. Below them were the dregs of humanity, thieves and worse rascals, preying on decent people.

"How do yuh aim to go about findin' this Tynsdale hombre?" inquired Naler, confused at the increasing bustle about them as they headed for the center of the city.

"I'm hopin' he may be so important folks will know him. I'll smell him out somehow."

A big dray laden with bales of cotton and drawn by four heavy horses thundered by them, driven by a cursing demon plying his whip and shrieking imprecations on anyone in the way. Naler's mettled horse reared and fought the bit and Naler had a session with his mount.

Evening was at hand. The low sun sent its spreading rays in golden splendor across Buffalo Bayou. On the shore stood many fine mansions, out of the way of the main bustle of the town.

Wagons and saddle horses blocked the cobbled streets. Drays and trucks passed both ways, pushing the riders to the gutter. Workmen and a mixed crowd of passersby were on the sidewalks, and the street lamps and lights in the saloons, restaurants and homes were coming on. Houston hummed with humanity and with action.

"There's a livery stable I went to before down this side street," said the Ranger, leading the way.

Pete's Stable stood on a quieter byway. It had a fenced yard with shade in the rear and plenty of stalls. Naler and Hatfield saw to their own horses, rubbing them down, and leaving strict orders as to watering and feeding.

Then the two tall young fellows walked toward the center of the city. Heedless and hurrying pedestrians bumped into them and they had to dodge drays and hansom cabs as they crossed the streets. They paused under a street light at a còrner and a couple of young women smiled and nodded to them.

"There's a big saloon up here called Tony's," said the Ranger. "They got the best free lunch in Texas. Come on." He was rather enjoying showing his friend Naler the sights.

Tony's Metropolis was a huge place and filled with drinkers. The long bar ran all the way through to the other block on one side and on the other stood tables heaped with delicacies for the customers to enjoy. Great roasts of beef, hams, corned beef, pork chops, pig's feet, tripe, sausages and oysters. There was liver, kidneys, clams and shrimp, hard-boiled eggs, potatoes and other vegetables. Also to be had was tongue, fried chicken, rolls and corn bread. Preserves, candies, and many other sweets, filled the boards.

Naler stared, astounded.

"Never see so much chow in all my born days! Where do yuh start?"

"Over here," said the Ranger drily, indicating the mahogany bar. "Yuh have to buy a drink first."

He nodded toward the burly bouncers who were unobtrusively watching for tramps and other raiders who might try to take food without the formality of purchasing at least a small beer.

They took their drinks to the free lunch counters and ate until they could not hold any more.

There was a dance floor through a wide opening. Hurdy-gurdy music banged from there and the building shook as couples bounced around to the lilting tunes. A female singer's brassy wail reached them:

I'm only a bir-rd in a gil-ded cahage . . .

The saloon hummed with men relaxing after the day's work. Tobacco smoke hung dense in the rafters. Upstairs were gambling rooms.

"Let's get outside," gasped Naler. "I need a breath of air."

"Wait for me on the porch. Be with yuh in a jiffy."

Hatfield went to the bar and signaled a bartender.

"What'll it be?" asked the aproned attendant.

"Yuh ever hear tell of an hombre by the name of Tynsdale?"

"Tynsdale? What's his first name?" The barkeeper turned away with a quick nod to serve another customer nearby.

When he came back, Hatfield replied, "Sidney."

"Sidney who?"

"Now wait a minute," ordered the Ranger. "I asked if yuh'd savvy Tynsdale, *amigo*."

"Oh, yeah, yeah. Huh. Tynsdale. I've heard the handle. Why don't yuh look in the city directory? The boss has one in the front office."

The directory was a help. It listed Tynsdale. Hatfield quickly memorized the information and rejoined Naler.

"What luck?" asked the rancher.

"Interestin'. Tynsdale is a manufacturer and has a factory on Front Street. He lives out on the Bayou shore. But we'll find a room and get some shut-eye. Start on Tynsdale in the mornin'."

They spent the night in a rooming house and were up and had breakfasted at an early hour. Picking up their horses they rode the miles to Tynsdale's factory, a long building made of red bricks sooted by the smoke from the big stacks. It was set off by itself in a large lot down the waterfront. The firm had a private railroad siding on which stood several cars. In a smaller, separate structure were the offices.

A large sign proclaimed the nature of the Tynsdale enterprises:

Workers were arriving and pouring in at the factory gates. Naler and Hatfield stayed back out of the way, across the street.

"There he is!" said the Ranger.

An equipage drove up and stopped before the office. The dark man of whom Naler had spoken to Hatfield, and, who was Felipe Palacio, jumped down and obsequiously assisted Sidney Tynsdale to the walk. Tynsdale wore a derby hat and a blue business suit. A diamond glinted in his necktie. He was carrying a stick with a jeweled head, and wore kid gloves.

"He shore dresses fit to kill," remarked Naler.

Palacio trailed his master inside. The lean, Spanish-looking man was wearing the same plain black suit and hat in which the Ranger had seen him before.

Hatfield watched the office door shut behind Palacio. He pushed back his Stetson and scratched his head. He could not as yet see what Tynsdale's game could be, attacking the people of the Yellow Hills. Here in the broad daylight of the bustling city, it was hard to believe that the elegant proprietor of the powder plant had any connection with Dowie Burke and the roster of death which Hatfield had come upon.

"Here goes," said the Ranger. "I'm goin' inside, Naler. You wait out here and don't show unless yuh hear me call."

CHAPTER XI

Lion's Den

Going across the street at a swift pace, the Ranger entered the Tynsdale & Co. office. He found himself in a short corridor with an umbrella stand and coat rack hemming him in. Ahead was an open door into a square anteroom and a young man sat at a desk watching him as he entered. There were benches around the room and pictures on the cream-colored walls.

Behind the young fellow on guard were two oak portals. On the one on the left a brass plate announced, "Mr. Tynsdale. Private." The other was marked "Offices."

"Good morning, sir." The clerk smiled as the tall man paused before him. "Are you Mr. Spoffendorf? You're early. Mr. Tynsdale just arrived."

"Yes, and it's him I want to see," replied the Ranger softly, thus evading the question.

He could hear voices behind the oaken doors. One seemed to come from Tynsdale's private office. It sounded like the dominating tones of the elegant bearded proprietor. Hatfield never needed to hear a man's voice but once, in order to recognize it again, and he had heard Tynsdale speaking at the Palace Hotel when the man had taken his leave.

The clerk rose from his desk and went to the left-hand door. He cleared his throat, took a deep breath and, raising his clenched hand, tapped in a gingerly, almost frightened manner as though rapping at the entrance to a lion's den. Presently a sharp voice said with an irritated ring: "Yes, yes, what is it? Come in."

The lithe Ranger had circled the desk and stood so that he would not be in line when the door opened. The young man turned the brass knob and stood at attention. "Sir," he said, "Mr. Spoffendorf is here."

"Very well," snapped the man in the office. "I'll be with him in a moment. Tell him to wait." He called loudly, "Palacio! Bring me the Spoffendorf correspondence at once."

The clerk smiled at Hatfield and seemed relieved that the ordeal of speaking to the lion in his den was over.

"Just a minute, sir."

It was but a brief wait until a bell tinkled and the clerk nodded to the Ranger. "You may go right in, sir."

Hatfield turned the knob and entered Tynsdale's office. He shut the door behind him and stood there, looking at his man. He had not had much time in which to study Tynsdale during the brief interlude at Stuart's Ford, but now the sunlight streamed in at the side windows and he had a real look at the stout master.

Tynsdale was perhaps thirty-five. Seated at the polished desk his paunch was hidden by the furniture. He had thin lips set between his brownish goatee and clipped mustache, discolored where numerous cigars had rubbed. Over his prominent cheekbones the flesh was taut and marred by little red blotches of broken veins, the high color of a gourmet and heavy drinker.

But after a searching overall look, it was Tynsdale's eyes which Hatfield fixed upon. They protruded like cold marbles and seemed to stab into the visitor. Myriad little wrinkles and lines radiated from the corners. They were the eyes of a ruthless and commanding personality who would stop at nothing, decided the Ranger.

"Sit down, Spoffendorf, sit down." Tynsdale essayed a smile, the seams of his face deepening. He took a fat cigar from a carved box and pushed the case across the desk. "Smoke up."

"Thanks, suh." The Ranger selected an expensive Havana and lighted it, but Tynsdale preferred to chew on his weed for a time. The man picked up a sheaf of papers. In baskets on the desk were many such reports and piles of correspondence.

"Look here," began Tynsdale with acerbity. "I'm a seller of powder and not here to give advice to the lovelorn rebels you represent. After this confine your letters to simple statements of fact. I'll furnish you a hundred or a thousand barrels of gunpowder, but the rights and wrongs of your case mean exactly zero to me. And I don't manufacture cartridges, but I can recommend a good firm. Sub rosa, of course, confidentially, just as this deal with me must be. There's a Federal law against gunrunnin'."

He shot a hard look at Hatfield and reached for a match to light his cigar.

"Since you intend to use this powder for breaching and such purposes," he went on, "I have had the percentage of sulphur increased to speed up the rate of burning. You have almost a blasting powder. You perhaps know that gunpowder is a mixture of charcoal, saltpetre and sulphur. The sulphur vapor spreads the flame through the charge.

"We have every facility here for large output. We make our own charcoal. The nitrate is imported and brought in ships to our own wharf. A cartel has got hold of most of the domestic sulphur supply and jacked the price, but I expect to solve that problem before long. At the moment I must charge more per barrel. You have the cash with you, I suppose. This sort of thing is always on the barrel head, of course."

The man was obviously a supplier of explosives and so long as he got his money he did not care where they went. At the time Hatfield knew of half a dozen wars going on throughout the world. There were rebellions to the south, across the Mexican border and in South and Central America, in Europe, and fighting in Asia and Africa. On the frontier were quarrels with Indians and be-tween large bands of white men as well.

Gunpowder was a coveted and vital necessity in all these disputes. Tynsdale was in a position to make quick fortunes with his factory.

As the Ranger turned this over in his mind he could hear the clock on the wall ticking.

"Come, come, Spoffendorf," Tynsdale snapped impatiently. "*Hora fugit*—time flies. If you wish to win you must be ready to strike hard and fast. *Periculum in mora*—there is danger in delay."

"Sorry, suh," drawled the Ranger. "But yuh got me mixed up with someone else. I ain't Spoffendorf. My handle is Hatfield."

Tynsdale started with such violence that his knees hit the underside of his desk. His eyes popped out and began to blaze.

"What! You're not Spoffendorf? Twill!"

He bellowed the clerk's name, and banged the bell at his hand.

"Take it easy," ordered Hatfield. "I want a word with you, Mr. Tynsdale." He put respect into his voice, for he wanted to impress the bearded man and not antagonize him until he could discover just what Tynsdale was up to in the Yellow Hills.

There was a timid tap on the door. Tynsdale was glaring at the interloper and rattling the sheaf of papers. The cigar revolved in his wet lips and he snorted angrily.

"I mean business," said the Ranger.

One slim hand rested close to the holstered Colt at his bunched hip and he moved the fingers tentatively, a play which Tynsdale did not fail to see.

"Tell him never mind," commanded Hatfield. "I don't want to hurt anybody if I can help it."

Some of the hot rage left Tynsdale and he grew more calculating as respect and fear for the armed young man before him took hold. There was an underlying threat to

76

Tynsdale in the soft drawl of the big fellow, and Tynsdale's eyes narrowed.

"Never mind, Twill," he sang out, and sat quiet.

"Just what is it you want?" inquired Tynsdale. "I'd be pleased to know why you posed as Spoffendorf to force your way in here."

"I didn't, suh. But that's neither here nor there. I'd have got to you one way or another."

Tynsdale was regarding him with corrugated brows.

"Have we met before?" he asked. "You have a familiar look."

"Never really met, but we were face to face one evenin' in Stuart's Ford."

Again Tynsdale was startled, and this time really alarmed. He tried to dissemble, repeating "Stuart's Ford, eh?"

"That's right. I just come from there."

Tynsdale waited, watching him. Hatfield noted that the man had fine white hands, too small for such a large man, as Tynsdale began to drum on the desk with two fingers of his right hand. One-two-three. One-two.

The thuddings were repeated. Unconsciously Hatfield's attention was caught by the diamonds that flashed in the gold settings of Tynsdale's rings and by the jeweled stickpin stuck in his white stock. His clothing was expensive and in the height of fashion.

A warning suddenly prickled the Ranger's spine. He was seated facing Tynsdale, and at his back was the small side door which led into the other offices. He hitched his chair around quickly, just in time to see the silent opening of that door. The morose figure of Palacio appeared.

"The cuss signaled him with his tappin'," decided the alert Ranger.

Tynsdale's furious eyes warned Palacio but too late for the big Ranger was up and had a Colt rising and cocked under his thumb.

"Come on in," ordered Hatfield.

The slim Palacio's dark face was sharp. His thin shoulders were stooped and his dark eyes were set in deep pits. They had a gloomy, glowing light. His arms were too long and yellow hands like claws hung at the ends of them. All in all he reminded the Ranger of a dangerous serpent.

Palacio said nothing, did not move. He saw the gun and his master frozen in his chair behind the desk. But he did not obey Hatfield's command.

"Tell him to step inside and close the door, Tynsdale. I don't aim to shoot, but the first slug goes for you if yuh force me."

Tynsdale knew this masterful tall man meant what he said.

"Come in and shut the door," he growled, and Palacio obeyed, standing in front of the door with his long arms relaxed at his slender hips.

"I'll get to the point," began Hatfield in a businesslike tone. "First off, I'm after the same thing you are, and that's money."

Palacio never took his burning eyes off the Ranger. Hatfield knew that under his black coat would be a pistol, and that no doubt he carried a knife as well. And Hatfield knew the man would die if need be to protect Tynsdale. Palacio was ready to spring.

"Yuh have heard that Dowie Burke lost out over there —you know where?" went on the Ranger. "A handful of farmers chased his bunch all the way to Jericho."

Hatfield carefully slipped his Colt back into the holster as he watched Tynsdale. He could tell that Burke's defeat was no news to the man for Tynsdale only gave a brief shrug. A curtain had been drawn across the glassy blue eyes, as Tynsdale simply waited to see and hear what would occur.

Probing at Tynsdale, Hatfield realized that his idea was correct. Dowie Burke was only a hireling, and while

78

dangerous in the field, could be dealt with. It was Sidney Tynsdale who was the real menace to the people about Stuart's Ford. If Burke died there would be others sent by Tynsdale to carry out his purposes.

"Burke is stupid," said the Ranger coolly, puffing at his cigar. "Why, he'd hardly got to work before those folks knew he was around and operatin'! They found Styles' body and Burke was beat off and nearly captured at Jordan's."

Tynsdale knew just what he was talking about. He was tense and he was growing more and more alarmed at the extent of the caller's information. But he was too shrewd to add anything to this fund and still waited without speaking.

Hatfield searched for a word, something that would nudge Tynsdale into exposing himself. He had a baffled feeling, for Tynsdale was hard to get at. Sure of his power, the powder magnate had a tough ego. He was silently struggling against the spell of the big fellow.

"Yuh want to get rid of certain men in the neighborhood of Stuart's Ford," said Hatfield flatly. "Ain't that right?"

Tynsdale only shrugged. "How long do you expect to keep jawin'?" he muttered, biting at his cigar. "I'm a busy man."

It was then that Jim Hatfield played his top card.

CHAPTER XII

Explosives

Reaching into his shirt pocket, Hatfield brought forth the smudged list of death. He unfolded it and slid it across the shiny desk top under Tynsdale's nose.

"Burke is so dumb," he said, "that he lost this and I got it. That's yore handwritin', Tynsdale."

The cigar traveled in frantic circles and Tynsdale would not look directly at Hatfield for a time. Then he said:

"Are you a law officer?"

The Ranger gave a surprised laugh.

"Shucks no! So that's what's eatin' yuh. Yuh figger I'm a snoopy sheriff on yore trail. Why, I'm here to join up with yuh if yuh'll have me. I told yuh all I want is to make money."

Both Tynsdale and Palacio seemed to feel better.

"Burke is all right as a gunslinger, but he has no finesse," continued the Ranger. "Yuh're a smart hombre and yuh must savvy that by this time. He's done for around Stuart's Ford. He only got two men on this list yuh gave him—old Styles and John Phelps. If he shows up there again they'll rise and tear him to pieces, and he might even squawk and fetch you into it if it come to that. I'm a different kind of Indian, Tynsdale. I'll guarantee to bring the jobs off for yuh without any fuss."

Tynsdale was growing interested. The earnest sureness and the flashing speed of the tall man before him could not fail to impress.

"Since you have the list," suggested Tynsdale, "why not go ahead and carry it out?"

"Would yuh pay me then? And if so how much?"

Tynsdale was silent again. He was troubled and kept darting glances at the bronzed, rugged face. He was a clever operator, thought Hatfield.

Hatfield kept trying. "Burke is no good to us any more and neither are his gunhands. They're all spotted over there."

For a moment he thought that Sidney Tynsdale meant to open up, but they were interrupted by a timid tap at the front door.

"Oh, Mr. Tynsdale," Twill called. "Mr. Burke is here."

Tynsdale looked at Hatfield. The play was up to the Ranger.

"Tell him to send Burke right in," ordered Hatfield.

He rose and glided to a point where the opening door would hide him from anyone entering. Tynsdale repeated his instruction to the clerk outside. Presently the door was pushed in and Dowie Burke came in, grinning widely.

Burke had on fresh clothing and wore his guns. He shut the door by kicking it with his heel and advanced toward the desk with his hand outstretched.

"Howdy, boss. Mighty good to see yuh. Yuh had my message? It was tough, but we did get Phelps and Styles."

Burke stopped smiling and paused in the middle of the velvet carpet to lick his lips. His blue-whiskered jaw stuck out, and he frowned.

Tynsdale put his hands behind his head and leaned back in his chair. He gave a brief nod at Hatfield and Dowie Burke slowly turned. His horrified gaze fixed on the Ranger, who was slouched against the wall. With a rat's squeak in his throat Dowie Burke went for his Colt.

But his blunt hand froze to the walnut stock of his heavy revolver. He knew when he was beaten and he knew the speed of Jim Hatfield when he wanted to show that his draw was blinding. Burke was staring into the black muzzle of the big Colt and he watched with fascination for the tall man's thumb to raise. That would be the end of Burke.

"Well?" snarled Burke at last.

"Let yore hands drop and sit down in that chair, Burke," said the Ranger contemptuously, and Dowie carefully obeyed. Tynsdale was savagely amused at Burke's discomfiture. Hatfield believed that the man must be angry at Burke's fumbling work.

"You fool, Burke!" said Tynsdale coldly. "You led this man to me. Suppose he should be a law officer?"

Dowie Burke gulped. He was fully aware of the big man standing behind him and was unable for a moment to offer any excuses.

"He even has the list I gave you," accused Tynsdale.

Burke jumped in his seat but took care not to make any move which might be construed as going for a weapon.

"So you was the one I had the fight with that night at Jordan's!" he cried.

"That was me, Dowie," boasted the Ranger. "Yuh're a jack."

Burke took in a gasp of air. He could see that his influence with Tynsdale and his own reputation as a tough were rapidly disintegrating.

"That big galoot there is a friend of Moss Jordan's and Ben Naler's," he yelled angrily. "He wrecked my game, Tynsdale! He saved Naler's life the other night in the Palace just when we had the cuss where we wanted him!"

"Shore I saved Naler," said the Ranger instantly. "He's my pardner. We're in business together."

"And what's your business exactly?" said Tynsdale.

"Hosses. There's some mighty fine ones at Jordan's, and we were after 'em. Fact is we aimed to run 'em off that night but Burke horned in on us. If yuh want a job done by real salty hombres, Tynsdale, yuh can't pick better men than Naler and me. We've operated all across Texas without bein' suspected."

"I'm not after horses," said Tynsdale drily. He was regaining his aplomb. He was sure now that the startling visitor must be an outlaw, who was seeking to enlist with him.

"Whatever yuh're after, yuh'll get it if yuh trust me," declared Hatfield.

Burke's ugly face was red and he was badly shaken. His stock had dropped to zero and he had lost what he considered a great thing, the confidence and pay of Sidney Tynsdale.

"*Humanum est errare*," said Tynsdale solemnly. "'To err is human,' but you have wrecked my plans, Burke."

"Yuh mean I'm through?" growled Dowie.

Tynsdale shrugged. "*Nous verrons ce que nous verrons*—we shall see. You're living at the same place?"

"Yes, suh."

"Go back there and hole up. I'll send you word soon."

Twill's voice reached them, alarmed and shrill.

"But you cannot go in there, sir. Mr. Tynsdale is busy."

"Got to, hombre," Naler's voice answered. "My pard's inside."

"Everything under control, Ben!" Hatfield called. He realized that Naler, having seen Dowie Burke enter, had grown worried and was trying to force his way in. To Tynsdale he said, "That's my pal, Ben Naler. He's all right—nothin' to worry about. Leave it all to us."

"Do I have to stay here?" snapped Burke.

"Nope," said the Ranger. "Go on. But keep out of my sight."

Burke rose and stalked out. He passed Ben Naler in the anteroom and gave Naler a scowl but hurried on. He bumped into a worried-looking middle-aged man in cowboy garb who was coming in.

"Mebbe I'm late," Hatfield heard that man say. "I'm Dave Spoffendorf. Got an appointment to see Mr. Tynsdale."

Hatfield felt that he had pushed Tynsdale as far as he could at the moment. Tynsdale would want to think it all over. The Ranger hoped he had impressed the gunpowder manufacturer and that Tynsdale would later take him into his confidence. But of this he could not be sure, for Tynsdale was a most wary person.

"S'pose I come back tomorrer, Mr. Tynsdale?" he said respectfully. "Yuh can decide by then what yuh want to do. I ain't the one to force myself on a feller."

Tynsdale blinked. He nodded and there was a narrowing of the marble eyes. Palacio watched Hatfield, not speaking.

"Where can I find you if I want you?" inquired Tynsdale, as Hatfield started out the door.

"Oh, I'll be around. Probably drink and eat at Tony's Metropolitan tonight."

As the Ranger left the private office Ben Naler was glad to see his tall comrade and gripped Hatfield's shoulder as they went outside.

"I was afeared Burke and Tynsdale might down yuh," he said in a low voice. "Hope yuh didn't mind me comin' in."

"That's all right, Naler. Burke come alone?"

"Yeah. There he goes."

Dowie Burke had mounted a yellow mustang and was moving up the street. He looked back and saw Naler and Hatfield, but only turned and kept going.

Naler and Hatfield crossed to their horses and mounted.

"Any luck?" Naler asked eagerly.

Hatfield shrugged. "I ain't shore yet, Ben. I did my best to impress Tynsdale, but he's as hard as the diamonds he sports. I could swear he's behind all that trouble, but I don't savvy why. That's one thing puzzles me. Another is how powerful an organization Tynsdale may have here in Houston. He hired Dowie Burke just for the work around the Yellow Hills. One thing's certain. We'll have to watch our step around town. Tynsdale ain't past havin' us taken care of."

They saw Burke put spurs to his horse and take the first corner. Evidently he was afraid that Hatfield and Naler meant to come for him. But the Ranger and his tall rancher friend showed no such signs as they moved away from the powder factory, which hummed busily, black smoke pouring from the chimneys. Hatfield rode in silence, his chin down.

"What now, Jim?" Naler asked presently.

"We'll hang around and take it easy today," said the officer. "A rest won't hurt either of us after the way we been goin'. Let Tynsdale simmer a while."

He had an uncomfortable sensation in the back of his neck and kept glancing around. The sunlight glinted on the windows of Tynsdale's office, but he could see nothing amiss. . . .

Houston hummed with antlike activity through the day. Hatfield and Naler did some sightseeing and napped in the hot afternoon. They partook of the sumptuous free lunch at Tony's Metropolitan and then went out again for a stroll when darkness was at hand.

Hatfield walked with no purpose for a time, deep in thought. He only grunted or nodded in reply to Naler's comments. At last the Ranger made up his mind.

"I'm goin' over to stable and pick up Goldy, Ben," he said. "I aim to visit Tynsdale's home and see if I can find out anything more. I don't feel comfortable."

"I'm with yuh," Naler promptly declared.

Hatfield had obtained the address of Tynsdale's mansion from the city directory. They went back to the livery stable and, saddling up, rode along the bayou highway. When they had left the city behind there were fine homes on the heights.

One of these was Sidney Tynsdale's. It stood in parked grounds and there was a high iron picket fence about it. Iron stags and other statues were placed about the carefully tended lawns. The front gate stood wide open and the big house was brightly lighted, but there was a uniformed attendant at the main entrance.

"Looks like Tynsdale is entertainin' this evenin'," remarked the Ranger as they rode on around the block.

CHAPTER XIII

Thumbs Down

Faintly the wind brought the strains of music from the mansion through the open windows, for the night was warm. The Ranger hunted a way inside the grounds, hoping to spot Tynsdale and learn something more about his quarry.

The high spiked fence Hatfield discovered ran all the way around the grounds. He and Naler were almost back to the front street before they came to the service entrance, a marked gate in the palisades, but this was locked and dark. However, the Ranger got an idea, as he looked up at the big oak tree whose limbs extended over the walk.

"Wait with the hosses across the street, Naler," ordered Hatfield. "I'm goin' in."

From Goldy's back it was easy to reach a strong limb of the oak and pull himself up and over the spikes. Naler then led Goldy across the road to the shadows of some scrub growth in the vacant lot there.

The silent Ranger picked spots of cover and flitted in. There were many sounds coming from the mansion—music, the buzzing hum of many people in laughing talk, the clatter of dishes in the kitchen. There was a banquet going on and in the big dining room a long table set with snowy linen and silver service was laden with good things to eat for Tynsdale's guests.

From his vantage point outside a French window giving into the big room, the Ranger could see the assemblage, the men in evening clothes and the ladies

86

gorgeous in silk gowns and jewels. At the host's position sat Sidney Tynsdale in faultless evening attire, his bearded face smiling. Wine was flowing and uniformed servitors passed silver platters of meats, vegetables, and various vintages.

Most of the male guests had the look which comes with power and importance, and some were plainly foreign. Hatfield could not make out much of the small talk but concluded that this was an affair which Tynsdale had given for business as well as social purposes. Such a man as the gunpowder manufacturer would need high contacts.

He did not see Palacio, but after he had been watching for a half-hour the lugubrious-looking bodyguard came through from the rear of the house and stood at Tynsdale's elbow. The man's master stopped his conversation, excusing himself, and followed Palacio through the swinging door.

"What now?" wondered Hatfield.

He moved along the stone wall, skirting the shrubbery, and reached more open windows. They gave into a library in a wing between the dining room and the kitchens. Here he located Tynsdale and Palacio, and Dowie Burke stood with his hat in hand before his employer.

"You shouldn't have come here, Burke," said Tynsdale sharply. "I told you that before. You gave me away once. What do you want?"

Burke was pleading and almost humble. "I wish yuh'd give me another chance, boss. I couldn't talk today with Naler and that big rascal around. But they're the ones wrecked us in the Yellow Hills. I'm enlistin' new men and I guarantee to bring it off right this time."

"You shouldn't have come here," repeated Tynsdale coldly. He took a cigar from a box on the table and lighted it as he thought. Then he said, "However, I'll give you another chance, Burke. You'll be at the same address, the one you gave me?"

"Yes suh," replied Burke eagerly.

"Go home now and wait for me. I'll be along to see you, probably around ten or eleven o'clock, as soon as I can get away from the party. We can talk at your place."

"*Bueno!*" cried Burke, and seized Tynsdale's hand, pumping it. "Yuh'll find I'll deliver the goods this time, boss."

"Do you know where Naler and the other one are stayin' in town?" inquired Tynsdale.

"No suh. I hope to find out, though. I tell you yuh can't trust either of 'em." Burke spoke earnestly.

Tynsdale put a hand on Burke's burly shoulder with bluff good comradeship.

"Run along, then. You came in by the service gate, Palacio tells me. The guard will let you out the same way. You must not be seen around here."

Dowie Burke nodded and went out. Tynsdale remained smoking in the library and when Palacio returned after seeing Burke out a side door the manufacturer said:

"Go to Vance at once, Palacio. Tell him to include Burke and his men. I'm through with the whole bunch."

The blue eyes bulged with icy coldness. There was a vicious look on Tynsdale's bearded face and the cigar twirled between his wet lips.

"*Pollice versa,*" he said, and put both thumbs down, the condemnation to death.

Palacio nodded and slipped away, his master returning to the banquet. . . .

Outside the Tynsdale grounds, Ben Naler had drawn well back out of sight with Goldy and his own horse. He had taken the precaution of muzzling his bay gelding for sometimes the horse would call to him when he left the animal standing. He had dropped the reins and gone to a point from which he could see the big oak tree and the service gate. He squatted in the shadows to await the Ranger's return.

Naler thought of all that had happened since he had left his ranch across the Pecos. He had crossed Texas and, having heard of Moss Jordan's elegant Kentucky horses, had reached Stuart's Ford and visited Jordan's. There his whole life had been changed. He mused on the strangeness of fate. Connie had first fascinated him, and now she held him with an invisible, unbreakable chain. He would never be the same carefree bachelor he had been when he had left home.

All his hopes now centered on the girl. Everything he planned in the future would include her.

"That is," he thought, "if she'll have me. I hope Hatfield is right. I wonder if I got a chance?"

When he had gone back to Jordan's after the first visit it had not been to argue over buying the thoroughbreds. There were other breeders. He had gone back because he could not stay away from Connie. He could picture her in his mind, her smiling eyes and the way the wind disturbed her golden hair.

"She's finished the dishes," he thought. "And she'll be sittin' there with her dad and mebbe Mrs. Phelps. Readin', I'll bet, or sewin'."

He had stayed to help Jordan in the fight against Dowie Burke, on account of Connie. And he was with Hatfield in Houston on the same score. But even so, some of it had been on the Ranger's account. Hatfield's power and ability had impressed Naler greatly. He would swear by and follow him anywhere, and admiration for the big officer filled him.

A horseman approached the service gate and Naler tensed, peering from behind his clump of brush. The rider looked around once, then dismounted and rang a bell which had a cord within reach of the outsider. There was something familiar about the caller's figure, but it was dark and Naler could not recognize the man.

After a while a lantern came into view and a uniformed guard held it up from inside the bars. The yellow rays shone on Dowie Burke's ugly features and Naler was sure then who the visitor was.

"I got to see Mr. Tynsdale," he heard Burke say. "It's mighty important. Tell Palacio if yuh want."

The gate was unlocked. Dowie Burke went inside and followed the bearer of the light toward the mansion.

Burke's appearance worried Naler, just as it had that morning. He wondered what Dowie wanted with Tynsdale, and if Burke might bump into Hatfield around the grounds. At last he crossed the road and moved to the gate. Burke's mustang stood with dropped reins in the gutter. Naler argued with himself on whether or not to try and follow the Ranger. Should he go over the fence and be ready in case Burke made trouble? But then he shook his head. Hatfield would be hidden and out of the light.

He could see Burke and the guard as they reached the back door of the mansion. Strains of music and louder talk and laughter came to Naler.

"I'll go back and wait like he told me to," he thought.

A faint sound caused him to look around quickly and his hand flew to his Colt. But it was too late. He got his left arm up enough so that it partially deflected the descending carbine barrel, but the steel cracked the side of his head and he went down with a startled grunt.

He was almost knocked out and unable to do more than gasp. Three men were on him and they fell heavily so their weight pinned him and knocked out his wind.

Then Naler blacked out and went limp. He remembered nothing more. . . .

When Ben Naler came back to life he was lying on a wooden floor with hands and ankles trussed. A lamp on a box table in the center of the room gave light. A big bed with a dirty blanket spread on it stood against the wall and there were some chairs, old clothing and other things about. It was a combination bedroom and sitting room. He could see through a door into a front chamber but this was unlit save from the opening between the two.

Tobacco smoke and whisky fumes filled the bedroom. The curtains were tightly drawn and it was stuffy. Naler was aware of several pairs of legs around the table.

He breathed heavily, then someone said:

"He's awake, Dowie."

Naler knew then that Dowie Burke's men had jumped him, tied him, and brought him here. Burke's face was red from liquor and heat as he came over to spurn Naler with a sharp toe.

"I got yuh at last," he growled. "Yuh're goin' to pay for what yuh've done."

There was no mercy in Dowie Burke. He hated Naler and would kill him at the drop of the hat. There were four more outlaws in the little shack and from sounds outside Naler thought this must be Houston.

"All I need now is that big galoot yuh travel with and then it will be perfect," rumbled Dowie. "I'll cook him, too. Yuh're goin' to help me catch him, Naler. Yuh'll tell me where Hatfield is and what yore game is. Yuh ruined me with Tynsdale, but I'll make up by showin' what yuh really are."

Burke's desire to reinstate himself in Tynsdale's good graces dominated him.

"Come on," he ordered. "Where's that sidewinder livin'? I want to take him tonight. We found yore hoss in the bushes but not his. He didn't go out to Tynsdale's, did he? Sent you to spy there, I s'pose."

At least they had not captured the Ranger, thought Naler. And somehow the golden sorrel had evaded them. Naler's gelding would have stood with his reins down but Goldy must have moved off when he heard strangers approaching, so Burke had concluded that Hatfield was not around. Burke, wanting to surprise Tynsdale by the capture of both Naler and the Ranger, had hustled to his city hideout with Ben Naler. Now he meant to nab Hatfield.

Naler's hands were fastened behind him and his limbs ached. He had lost his hat and they had taken his guns. But he was still stubborn and would not answer Burke's questions as to his partner's whereabouts.

"All right," said Burke. "I'll show yuh. One of my grand-pappies was an Apache. I learned some tricks from the old fool. Gag him, Bert!"

CHAPTER XIV

Missing Pard

Dowie Burke's eyes burned his hate of Naler. He blamed his failure in the Yellow Hills entirely on the rancher and on Hatfield.

An outlaw tied a kerchief tightly across Naler's mouth and Burke picked up a long steel pin and held it over the lamp chimney. When it was glowing red-hot he thrust the point into Naler's cheek. A spasm of pain made the victim writhe. Burke pricked him in several places before the pin cooled. Then Dowie went to reheat it. As he held it over the lamp he talked to Naler.

"At first yuh'll tell yoreself yuh're too tough to crack, Naler. Yuh'll stand it. But each sizzle of yore flesh takes a little more out of yuh. After while yuh'll be weak as a kitten. Then I'll start on yore eyes. I'll blind one and if yuh don't talk by then I'll blind the other. I'll take yuh to pieces, bit by bit. No man could stand it. Yuh'll be cryin' like a baby soon."

He finished heating the pin and Naler could feel the

terrible jab of it even before Dowie used it. Squatted over the rancher, Burke made a tentative threat of jabbing his eyes. Naler closed them and turned his head aside. Dowie laughed.

"I'll have somethin' to deliver to the boss tonight," exulted Burke. "Yuh might as well squawk, Naler. I'll get yore pard sooner or later anyway and yuh can save yoreself a lot of torture by talkin'. Where's he livin'? You savvy. What's the game? Just who is he, and what's he doin' in this?"

Naler set his soul to stand anything. He would not betray his friend, but Burke had been right. He could feel himself growing weaker with each spasm of pain, as Dowie punctured his skin with the hot needle.

"Now for the first eye," Burke said grimly, as he again heated the pin.

A strip of thick leather wound around the cooler end of the pin protected Burke's blunt fingers. Dowie turned and brought the red-hot point slowly toward Naler's left eye, and again Naler turned his head away.

"Hold his ears, Fan," said Burke, and one of the outlaws roughly gripped Naler and wrenched the rancher's head around.

A loud knocking at the street door made them jump.

"See who it is," commanded Burke.

The man called Bert glided through to the outer room. Dowie pushed the connecting door part way to and they stood ready with their pistols. Voices came from up front. Then Bert came back.

"It's all right, Dowie," he reported. "It's an hombre with a message from Tynsdale."

"*Bueno.*" Dowie set the pin on a dish and strode out. His men trailed him.

Naler lay behind the table on the floor and the big bed bulked close at hand. The connecting door stood at right angles and cut off Naler's vision as far as the front door went.

It was a respite but a brief one, thought the rancher, his cheeks burning from the smarting punctures.

"Vance?" he heard Burke saying inquiringly, "Is Tynsdale comin'?"

There was a sudden hoarse cry and heavy guns began to roar. The burst of sound was overwhelming and stunning. A man screamed, but only once.

Ben Naler was aware of the terrific commotion in the outer room. He rolled himself over with the spasmodic desperation of self-preservation, back under the wide wooden bed and lay there panting, with his body pressed to the wall.

His shift of position made it possible for him to see a section of the front room's floor, although the low sideboard of the wide bed cut off the view so he could only take in the moving men as far as their knees. He could make out two bodies lying on the mat and the unmoving black boots of a third. They looked like Burke's bunch.

The front door was wide open. The running pairs of legs came toward him, several charging men, and their weight shook the wooden shack. A couple came swiftly through to check the bedroom.

"Empty," growled one. "We got 'em all, Vance."

A hard voice, a leader's curt tones, ordered: "We'll burn the place down."

One man swept the oil lamp from the table. Naler saw it crash and the glass reservoir, filled with kerosene, cracked open. The oil ran out on the floor but the lighted wick doused out. Matches were struck and touched to the pool of spreading oil which flared up and caught flaming hold.

"Two constables just come around the next corner, Vance," warned a lookout from the open door.

"Come on!" said Vance. "Let's get out before the law gets here."

The fire was picking up and licking at the wooden wall. The straw mat was ablaze. The voice of the fire increased, an ominous *whooshing* which grew toward a roaring threat of death. Smoke was drifting on the drafts.

The booted legs flashed away and vague shouts came to the confused Naler, tied, and under the bed. . . .

While Ben Naler was facing a death from torture, Jim Hatfield had spent over an hour out at Tynsdale's mansion. After Palacio had been ordered to have Burke killed by someone he called Vance, the lugubrious Spaniard had saddled a fleet horse and left by the front gates.

The Ranger did not know where Burke was living and he knew he could never get back to Goldy and trail Palacio in the night. He concluded that the Vance mentioned by Tynsdale must be a strong-arm merchant who worked for the gunpowder manufacturer. Burke would have to take his chance.

Hatfield went back to the window looking in on the banquet hall and saw Tynsdale resume his chair and smilingly entertain the company. One course after another came on—appetizers, soup, fish, entree, main course, desserts, with wine to accompany each, and cordials and cigars for the gentlemen after the ladies had retired to the drawing room. Tynsdale appeared to be set for the evening.

At last the Ranger left his post of observation and picked his line of retreat.

He went up the dark side of the big oak and sat for a few moments in the lower branches, scanning the road and side street, making sure all was clear. He saw nobody, and his eyes hunted for Naler for a time.

"He's keepin' well hid," he thought approvingly.

Dropping to the sidewalk outside the high iron fence the Ranger flitted across to the black area of brush and trees. He was sure Naler would hail him in a second for, if watching, Naler would surely have seen him coming.

Hatfield glanced back and, keeping down low, gave a low hail.

"Ben!"

There was no answer. Hatfield was mildly puzzled and kept going. Perhaps Naler had gone back to keep the horses quiet. He moved into the thickets, peering through the dark lanes. The Ranger knew that Naler would have led the animals well back out of sight of the road.

He paused and once more called in a sharp undertone: "Ben! Naler, where are yuh?"

Listening intently, all he could hear were muted strains of music and a far-off chatter of voices from Tynsdale's party in the great mansion.

Hatfield squatted in the center of the little woods, and stroked his chin. Then he began casting about, hunting Naler. It was possible that the rancher might have dozed off, waiting for him. But he could not locate the man. Nor could he find the horses. Had Naler grown alarmed by something and ridden off, with Goldy in tow?

All the way through the patch of brush and low trees, Hatfield turned back and tried again. He essayed a quick whistle. He listened intently and caught the sound of trotting hoofs coming toward him. He whistled a second time, and soon Goldy broke through to him and nuzzled his hand.

"Where's Naler, Goldy? What happened?"

But the golden sorrel only sniffed, glad to see his friend.

It was a puzzle, and Hatfield was alarmed. It was not like Naler to desert him.

"Mebbe he saw Dowie Burke and follered him," he mused, thinking it out.

Should he wait for the rancher, or move on? He glanced toward the mansion. He could see the brightly lighted windows through the branches.

For half an hour he hung around, hoping Naler would return. Impatient at the delay he went back over the spiked fence by jumping up and getting hold of a branch of the oak.

The party was still going on. They had finished dinner, and dancing had begun in the ballroom. Tynsdale, his bearded face wreathed in smiles, was dancing with a stout bejeweled lady. There seemed to be no alarm, nothing to indicate that Naler had been captured and brought to Tynsdale.

Hatfield returned to Goldy. He decided that Naler must have trailed Dowie Burke.

Naler would never quit except for a reason such as this.

"We'll go back to the city and he'll come home when he's good and ready," the Ranger murmured to Goldy.

He considered the possibility that Naler might have been jumped and downed. If so, they had found his horse and taken him along. Had he been certain that Naler was a prisoner he would have gone back and tried to capture Tynsdale, anything to force the issue, make Tynsdale tell where Burke could be located in case Dowie had managed to pick up Naler. But he was sure of nothing.

Mounting, the Ranger rode back to the center of the city. He smoked as he went, and the moon gleamed on the restless waters of Buffalo Bayou. Houston was warming up downtown as the revelry of night grew livelier and livelier.

Hatfield rode along a wide avenue. Off to his left he noted a red glow lighting the night sky.

"Looks like a house afire," he muttered and debated on whether to go watch the blaze or not.

But he was weary and wanted a drink. The fire was somewhere in the slums behind the waterfront, and a long ride from where he was.

Just on the chance that Naler might have gone home, Hatfield went around by way of the furnished room they

97

shared, but his friend had not come in. So the Ranger rode on toward Tony's Metropolitan. Naler would show up there for a drink and a snack if the rancher went anywhere before going home.

The street was crowded with saddle horses and with fine carriages and buggies. He had to leave Goldy halfway up the long block from Tony's. He ducked under the rail, went up the sidewalk, and turned into the bar.

It was filled with men. Busy aproned attendants served the customers. Glasses clinked and liquor flowed. Talk was loud and there was dancing going on, and gambling upstairs. The saloon was bright and warm and, after buying a long drink, Hatfield visited the free lunch counters. He kept looking around for Ben Naler, but did not see his comrade.

Uneasy, and growing more and more so as Naler failed to appear, Hatfield had a couple of drinks.

Behind the long bar which ran through from street to street, entrances at both ends of the building, were gleaming mirrors reaching to the ceiling. Racks of bottles of every known brand of "poison" stood on the mahogany shelves. There were cigars and pipe and chewing tobacco, matches, toothpicks, and fruits, all that might be desired by a finicky and thirsty customer. The cuspidors were shining brass.

It was decidedly pleasant at the Metro, but the atmosphere brought Jim Hatfield no relief.

CHAPTER XV

Clash

It was Hatfield's custom to go on the assumption that he might be in danger at all times. He was ever wary, especially when working on such a case as this. He knew that Sidney Tynsdale was a dangerous opponent, and Houston was Tynsdale's bailiwick.

Tynsdale had sent orders to someone called Vance. Hatfield did not recognize this name. He thought the man must be a local aide of the manufacturer's.

But the Metro was so open and so filled with people that he did not believe anything would be tried in the place. Still, he had mentioned the saloon to Tynsdale as a spot he frequented.

He managed to push in and get a place at the bar, a booted foot on the rail and an elbow hooked over the high counter. He was jostled, but it was all good-natured. The man next him began to talk about the weather, and the price of beef.

A couple more fellows came in but Hatfield barely noticed them, for men were leaving or entering all the time. There was great bustle and noise in the Metro. Hatfield munched a beef sandwich he had brought over from the tables and sipped his drink, exchanging remarks with his bar acquaintance.

The two new arrivals, however, had brought news, which passed along the bar. Hatfield listened as it was relayed down the gossipy line.

"Big fire out on Second Street," said his neighbor, who had caught the talk. "Cabin burned to the ground and they say it was full of dead men! Must have been a fight between two gangs. They're mighty bold in town these days. I don't know what the world's comin' to." The middle-aged city dweller shook his head solemnly.

More details came along. The police had made an arrest. Hatfield thought it over. He had seen the glow of the fire in the night sky as he had ridden back into Houston. It was the fact that men had been shot down that held him. Tynsdale had ordered Dowie Burke's extinction. Could it have been Burke and his gang who had died out there in the burning cabin? The timing would check with this assumption.

In the mirror he saw a six-foot-tall man in a black suit and hat, white shirt and string tie come in through the door by which the Ranger had entered. The fellow had a startling beard, black as ink and bristling like a porcupine's quills. It fanned out from his chin. If he wore a gun it was under his coat. He had keen, narrowed black eyes, and a hooked nose. There was something about his whole attitude and look which held the Ranger.

"Looks tough," he decided.

Behind Blackbeard came half a dozen more men. Some wore riding garments, others city clothing. They paused and waited as the man with the whiskers looked through the saloon.

"Huntin' somebody," decided the Ranger.

He was troubled, worried over Naler. The news that had come through about the fight and the burning cabin further alarmed him. Was it possible that Burke had captured Naler? If Naler had trailed Dowie and his bunch he might have been present when the shooting occurred, even if he was not a prisoner.

The next instant he glimpsed Palacio's lean figure and solemn dark visage. Palacio was pointing a bony finger at him from the doorway. The secretary had just come in, and stood beside Blackbeard.

The bearded man whipped a hand inside his jacket.

He had a pistol in a shoulder holster and was reaching for it. Hatfield knew instantly they had come after him. No doubt that other task set Vance by Tynsdale was to find Hatfield and Naler and kill them. And this black-bearded killer must be Vance.

The Metro was jammed with people. Bullets flying would hit innocent bystanders, and Hatfield was not a man to hurt decent citizens. He could not fire into Vance and Palacio without starting a burst from the drawn guns of the toughs who backed up their chief.

To draw fire from the crowd and to get some sort of bulwark between himself and the enemy guns, the Ranger acted with terrific speed. He threw himself across the bar, kicking out of the way the man he had been talking with and swiping several glasses and bottles off the counter. They crashed to the floor.

The bearded man's gun blasted and a bullet furrowed the mahogany. Several more men opened up and a customer close to where Hatfield had been standing screamed and sagged, gripping his slashed shoulder. The bullets made small holes in the great mirrors, holes with little cracks radiating from them.

The stampede began as men sought to get away from the blazing guns of the toughs blocking the doors. Behind the bar Hatfield was comparatively safe for the moment. The barkeepers shouted at him but ducked as they heard the zipping lead.

The bar was high enough so that Hatfield could move, stooped over. He wanted to get outside and save others in the saloon from stray lead. He bobbed up and saw Vance and his men moving toward the curving end of the bar from which point they could sweep the aisle and kill him. He had to shoot to slow them. His bullet knocked the bearded fellow's hat off, and made the leader wince and duck.

It was Hatfield's intention to rush out by the opposite exit, to the next block. He was two-thirds down the bar aisle when his heel caught in something and threw him hard on the wet walk behind the bar. It was an iron ring in a trap door.

He was up quickly, Colt in hand. Close by him was a quivering fat bartender, scrunched under the bar where copper tubing came up from the basement. The Ranger bobbed up again to see to Vance and his crew.

He fired once and a bullet cut his hat crown and smacked into the mirror. But it came not from Vance's side but from the other doorway toward which Hatfield was headed. A number of killers had crushed in that way and were after him. There were no windows on the bar side and he was trapped behind the long mahogany counter!

It was pandemonium in the saloon. Men were crying out in agony as they were crushed in the stampeding mob. A confused roar rose and the lamps shook on their gilt chains.

Hatfield was aware by now that Vance would stop at nothing to carry out Tynsdale's orders. The black-bearded man was utterly ruthless and would strike with smashing power, no matter where. Hatfield was caught between the two bunches of gunslingers, boring in on him. He had only seconds left, for even if he downed a few, they would kill him by sheer weight of numbers.

He whirled and jumped back the way he had come. He had to send a quickie at the bar end for he saw Vance and another man there taking aim at him. Then he reached down, gripped the iron ring, and jerked.

The heavy trap door came up and showed a flight of ladderlike steps going into the cellar.

The Ranger did not hesitate at going down the hatch.

He slipped and went sliding all the way to the bottom, fetching up on a packed dirt floor.

A wet, musty smell greeted his nostrils. There were liquors and casks of beer stowed down here. He could see faint outlines of small windows high up in the walls of the foundation. Overhead the floor of the saloon shook with stamping feet.

Hoarse yells and the roar of the crowd came from above.

He moved a few steps and ran into some cases. He took time to strike a match and the flare showed the big storeroom filled with bottled goods and barrels. An open door led him on into another room where there were more supplies of food and various types of equipment used by Tony's Metro.

He tried another match. A rat as large as a kitten scurried across his boot and disappeared among the boxes.

A shout and a whirling slug told him it was dangerous to strike any more matches. Vance and his boys had followed him.

The basement was large. Over on the far side he found a door which led into an enclosed place. Overhead showed a narrow patch of sky. He charged up the stairs and turned into the side street. It went through to both avenues and the Ranger picked up his feet and ran for it.

He slowed, with his gun up, as he came to the turn. Men were jamming the veranda of the Metro and staring through the open door and the windows at the scene inside. They blocked off Hatfield's enemies. He came out, pushed to the curb, and ducked under the rail.

He ran up the block at full speed and picked up Goldy's reins, springing to his saddle.

His breath rasped in his throat and a slow trickle of blood came from the gash in his scalp. He had felt a sting during the fight in the bar but he had been too busy to take much note of it. A splinter of glass also had jabbed him, and he found he had other scratches and cuts in his face and hands.

He saw Vance and his men surge from the alley. They glimpsed him as he passed under a street lamp but he was moving fast and their following lead went wide.

Hatfield made the next corner and took it, his speed increasing, the sorrel springy under him.

The Ranger drew in the night air, pulling himself together. His breath came in heaving gasps and he was badly shaken. Vance's attack had been most savage, and Hatfield had had little warning of it.

In the dark he was able to shake off the killers but they kept blindly pushing along, and soon he realized that Vance had riders on several parallel avenues so he could not double back on them. Twice patrols sighted him and whooped it up, calling to their comrades and shooting at the man on the sorrel.

He was jostled to the western limits of Houston before he managed to work over and lose them entirely.

Anger burned in him, but emotion was not good for clear thought and therefore he stifled it.

"Tynsdale is real sore," he thought. "He's wipin' the slate clean and aims to start over, using this Vance hombre. Tynsdale is smart, and Vance is mighty salty."

Sidney Tynsdale had been clever, the way he had led both Dowie Burke and Hatfield into believing he would use them as his allies. But Tynsdale had given his orders to have Burke and the tall man wiped out. Tynsdale was playing safe. Burke had shown himself to be a dull-witted fool who was dangerous to such an operator as the manufacturer, while Tynsdale would not trust the supposed horse thief who was trying to force his way in.

CHAPTER XVI

"Leave No Stones Unturned"

Undoubtedly Hatfield would have felt better had he known what had happened to Ben Naler. Vance, of course, was looking for Naler, and the Ranger knew what that meant, for it had taken every ounce of his own fighting ability to escape the smashing strike of the Houston bunch. If they bumped into Naler, the rancher would die.

Back in the Yellow Hills waited Connie Jordan, waited for Ben Naler to return. And Jordan and the inhabitants of the hills must have powerful assistance if they were to survive this next attack by Tynsdale, spearheaded by Blackbeard Vance.

The Ranger made a wide detour to evade possible far flung outriders of Vance's party and approached the lighted city from the south, pressing back to the heart of town. He knew he was a marked man now and liable to be shot on sight by Vance's men. In daylight he would have little chance of surviving for any length of time, for drygulchers with loaded rifles, hidden in buildings and niches outside them, could pick off any horseman.

"I've got to force a break," he decided, his keen mind working at full speed. "Tynsdale is at the head of it all. I'll try for him and before the new day breaks!"

He considered enlisting the Houston police force. They would cooperate with a Texas Ranger even though there might be some professional jealousy. Yet he was aware that such an influential citizen as Sidney Tynsdale would command political forces in the city, and would be a hard man to convict and hold. There would be bail, lawyers fighting, and time would run out. Meanwhile Tynsdale's agents could operate as they pleased and the Ranger might have his hands tied, his countering of Tynsdale exposed.

Again he neared the furnished room house where he had been staying with Naler. There was a chance that Tynsdale knew where it was, so Hatfield left Goldy around the corner and approached with every precaution. He wanted to see if Naler had come home. But the place was dark and there was no sign either of his friend or his enemies.

The Metro had quieted down but he did not go within two blocks of the place. He had made up his mind as to his next play and as usual it was bold, direct, and if it succeeded it might ease the whole situation.

The Ranger headed once more for Sidney Tynsdale's home. He hid Goldy back in the wooded fields and flitted close to the margin of them, peering over at the spiked fence and the big oak by which he had crossed the fence early in the night. It was late and Tynsdale's guests were leaving in elegant equipages. The main gates stood wide open and armed watchmen saluted as each carriage went past.

He drew back and froze close to the ground as riders came to the service gate across the road. He could identify Palacio's lean figure on a big black horse and as the man beside the dark-skinned secretary looked around, Hatfield saw that he wore a spiked black beard.

"Vance!" he thought.

Palacio opened the service gate with a big iron key and the two went through together. They trotted their horses up the winding gravel driveway toward the rear of the mansion.

The Ranger looked carefully at the shadowed area to the right, from which direction the pair had come. It was probable that Vance had men with him and they would surely see the Ranger if he crossed to the oak.

Silently he moved away and, keeping parallel to the long fence, reached the corner of it. It was dark enough so he could cross the street which he did, and he pressed against the black spikes.

He had left his big Stetson behind and dirt rubbed on his face killed the sheen of his skin. Girding himself, he put a toe between the spikes on the narrow joining piece at the bottom. This raised him high enough so he could get hold of the spearlike tops of two uprights. With his strong arms he drew himself up and though his shirt was torn and he was bruised about the ribs he managed to get over the high palings and dropped to the ground inside.

Reconnoitering, he found Palacio and Vance seated in the study between the kitchens and the dining room. They were drinking and smoking and waiting for Tynsdale, who was saying good night to the last of his dinner guests.

After twenty minutes of waiting Sidney Tynsdale came into the room. The manufacturer's face was grim.

"Well?" he snapped.

"We did somethin', suh," reported Vance. "We got Dowie Burke and his bunch. They're cooked and I mean shore enough cooked for we fired the shack and they burned up. Not one escaped."

"Good work!" exclaimed Tynsdale. He selected a fat cigar and thrust it between his bearded lips.

"Burke didn't have too many brains," said Vance with contempt in his voice. "He fell hook, line and sinker, and it wasn't too hard. He was mighty stupid, chief."

Tynsdale winked and said lightly, "*De mortuis nil nisi bonum*—of the dead say nothing but good, Vance! But you're right. Burke made a lot of trouble for me. How about Naler and Hatfield?"

Palacio spoke quietly. "We have not found the rancher, señor. But the tall devil has been wounded."

"We ran the cuss out of town," boasted Vance. "I'll

take him, I guarantee it, Mr. Tynsdale. Set yore mind at rest on that score. He hasn't got a chance. If he shows in Houston again he'll die."

Tynsdale's eyes snapped as he heard of the fight at Tony's Metropolitan.

"But the big one is dangerous," he protested. "He understands now it is *guerre à outrance*. Yes, war to the uttermost. *Nemo me impune lacessit.* No one attacks me with impunity."

"I'll get him," promise Vance. "Write him off. And Naler too."

"*Omnem movere lapidem*—leave no stone unturned," ordered Tynsdale. He loved to impress others with his erudition.

Hatfield crouched beside the open window of the study, hidden in ornamental shrubbery fringing the stone foundations of the great mansion. He could not capture Tynsdale with Vance and Palacio present, and with armed servitors on call.

"I wish to finish up a matter begun in the Yellow Hills, Vance," said Tynsdale. "I gave Dowie Burke a list of property holders there that I wanted put out of my way. It's vital. Burke wrecked the game with his blundering and brought Hatfield and Naler upon my head, as you understand. I must strike in the hills at once. How many men do you command?"

"As many as yuh want," replied Vance. "I only have a couple dozen regulars, but I'll hire as many extras as yuh say. I pay two dollars a day but this job shouldn't run more than a week or so."

"Get fifty or sixty," said Tynsdale. "I don't want any more slips."

Blackbeard Vance was very sure of himself. "I'll fix up the damage Burke done," he declared. "I'll settle their hash in the Yellow Hills. Yuh want me to wait and get Hatfield and Naler before I start over there?"

Tynsdale shook his head quickly. "It's possible that

either one may leave Houston and return to warn Jordan and the others about me. I wouldn't put it past them to sell out to those yokels for a price, to spite me. So we must start within twenty-four hours. This time I'll go along so there will be no mistakes."

"Whatever yuh say, suh. But I wish yuh'd come to me first instead of trustin' Dowie Burke."

"At the time it seemed best to use a roving gang such as Burke commanded," explained Tynsdale. "A friend sent Burke to me, and Dowie wanted work. He and his boys were range riders and it fitted in for the job."

Palacio started, and glanced toward the closed door. He raised a long finger to his lips and silently tiptoed to the door. But as he put a hand on the knob a loud rap came and a liveried servant stood waiting as the aide opened up.

"There's a man here to see Mr. Vance, sir."

Vance went out, leaving Palacio and Tynsdale together.

"What do you think of Vance?" asked Tynsdale.

"Señor, I think he is very good just now for us. Later I can't say. He is strong-willed."

Tynsdale nodded. "If Vance goes too far later I'll find a way to check him. *Est modus in rebus.* There is a limit in all things, Palacio."

"Yes, señor."

"I'll be glad to have this affair settled," went on Tynsdale, twirling his cigar between his wet lips. "It's a radical proceeding, but the surest and quickest method."

"Also the cheapest," murmured Palacio, with a nod.

"Yes, it should be. There's no saying what might happen if I'd let our secret slip. I'd be held up for a fortune and might even lose out entirely." Tynsdale was thinking aloud, spinning his ambitions into realities. "It will make a tremendous difference once I've won in the Yellow Hills. I'll command the industry. I'll rival Gould and Vanderbilt. I'll be really big. The world will point with envy at Sidney Tynsdale. I'll settle wars and other great affairs. And why should I care about the fate of a few stupid little people? The end justifies the means. *Exitus acta probat.*"

Vance came hurrying back into the room, his cheeks red with excitement where the flesh showed over the bristling beard.

"More good news!" he cried. "My men have located Ben Naler."

"Where is he?" demanded Tynsdale.

"In the city hall lockup," replied Vance. "Rumors were all around about Burke and his bunch and the fire of course. One man said the police had taken a prisoner. The place looked empty when I was in but we were pushed and couldn't hunt around. They say that a man was hidden under a bed, that he was tied up but rolled out into sight when the police and firemen arrived. They pulled him out just in time."

"So that's what happened to Naler!" thought the startled Hatfield.

"Why are they holding Naler?" inquired Tynsdale, scowling with puzzled attention.

"Just to check on him, I reckon. I s'pose he's told who he is. Mebbe even mentioned you."

Tynsdale made his decision. He turned to Palacio.

"Ride at once to Judge Swale's," he ordered. "Wake him up and tell him I want a habeas corpus writ at once for Ben Naler. Any name will do. I want a magistrate at the city hall within one hour, understand? We'll get Naler out before he has time to do much damage and before someone beats us to it."

Palacio glided away. "That leaves only the tall one," said Tynsdale to Vance. "Luck's with us tonight. Perhaps we'll get Hatfield before we start for the Yellow Hills. I'll see to Naler. You hustle and make your men ready for the ride."

"Yes, suh." Vance was breezily self-confident.

Tynsdale handed him a roll of bills and Vance went out, Tynsdale disappearing somewhere in the big house. Hatfield knew he must not linger. He had little time in which to save Ben Naler, for once Tynsdale had the rancher Naler would be done.

He flitted through the shrubbery and beautiful gardens to cross the high fence. Picking up the golden sorrel, he rode back to the center of Houston and straight to the main police station at the city hall.

A police sergeant at the desk glanced up at the grim face of the tall visitor.

"What is it now?" asked the sergeant gruffly.

Hatfield's clothing was torn and stained and while he had cleaned his face as best he could he was scratched and bruised. But the next minute the policeman jumped. He was looking at the silver star on silver circle, emblem of the Texas Rangers. Hatfield shoved credentials across the desk.

"And what can we do for the Rangers?" asked the sergeant, with new respect in his voice.

"Yuh got a prisoner here named Ben Naler. He was picked up at Burke's shack, the one that burned down earlier tonight. Yuh'll have to release him. I'll guarantee him."

"Well now, yuh ought to have a paper for him." The sergeant consulted the book. "He's held on suspicion. We were goin' to turn him loose in the mornin' if nothin' come up against him. Says he's an honest rancher and was set upon by a passel of outlaws."

"That's right. Is the chief of police here? Tell him I want to see him."

"The chief's home between the blankets, Ranger. I booked Naler meself. Let's see." The sergeant scratched his head. "Tell yuh what. I'll let yuh have him if yuh'll guarantee to produce him in the mornin' when court holds."

"*Bueno.*"

CHAPTER XVII

Rush

Minutes later the bedraggled Naler stood in the anteroom. He shook hands with Hatfield and began to tell him in an excited voice of his experiences. Hatfield cut it short, thanked the sergeant, and led Naler outside.

"We got no time to waste, Ben," he said. "Tynsdale's on the prod. Where's yore hoss?"

"I think the police fetched him here. He may be around back at their racks."

They rounded the brick building and there was Ben Naler's long-legged gelding standing at the hitch-rail. He was still saddled, as he had been brought in after Naler had been arrested. Naler checked the cinches and threw a long leg over the saddle. The Ranger was already mounted and they moved back on the lane at the side of city hall.

"Here comes Palacio!" warned the Ranger. "Keep back, Naler."

They waited in the shadow of the brick wall while Palacio and a small man in a blue coat who looked as though he had just jumped out of bed, went hurrying up the stone steps in front.

"They're after you," said Hatfield. "Aimed to take yuh out and finish yuh. Let's ride!"

Naler trailed him and they made fast time away from there for they could hear the sergeant roaring into the street from the front door, ordering them to come back. Frightened by the developments, the sergeant wanted the prisoner back. Glancing over his shoulder Hatfield saw Palacio, the sergeant, and Tynsdale's attorney shaking their fists after the running pair.

"Where to?" asked Naler.

"We'll pick up our gear on the way out and head for the Yellow Hills. Houston's too hot for us and we got to carry warnin' to Jordan and his friends."

They lost a few minutes as they paused at their furnished room and packed their sacks, picking up their carbines and the belts for them which had been left in the room when they had ridden into the city. Then Hatfield left a bill to pay the rent and they hurried out. Picking up speed, they made for the southwest trail.

Naler was worn to a frazzle and the Ranger needed a rest, but they put several miles between themselves and Houston before they pulled up and turned off the highway. There they hunted a spot where they could sleep a little while. They would make better time if they did not wear out themselves and their horses.

There was a small wooded mound overlooking the road and they made for it, hiding themselves and their mounts in the low growth. . . .

Dawn woke the Ranger. The sun was gilding the eastern sky and he rose and stretched. Ben Naler stirred uneasily in his sleep.

Hatfield felt refreshed. He took a drink of water from his canteen and rolled a quirly, thinking over what he must do. There was no use in applying to the Houston authorities, for Tynsdale had influence and the money to buy clever lawyers who could delay everything. The Ranger could not take such a chance, with the people of the Yellow Hills in danger of death. He must get back there and warn that Tynsdale and Vance were coming.

Through habitual alertness the Ranger scanned the highway stretching for miles in either direction. Houston could be made out to the northeast as the morning breeze dispelled the haze from the bayou. Dust rolled in a large cloud over the road coming from the town and he knew at once that a band of horsemen were coming along the pike toward him.

He brought out his field glasses and focused them. He did not look for long, but with a quick exclamation jumped over to shake Naler awake.

"Get up, Naler! Tynsdale, Vance and about fifty gun-hands are comin'!"

Warned by Naler's escape and the police sergeant's story that the tall man was a Texas Ranger, Tynsdale had jumped the gun and started early, aware that he must strike instantly if he wished to triumph!

By the time Goldy and Naler's gelding were saddled, though the enemy party had approached close enough so that the Ranger and his friend could not emerge and reach the road without being recognized.

Hatfield made his decision. "I'd rather they didn't savvy we're ahead of 'em, Naler. We'll stay hid till they pass. If Tynsdale sights us he may push on even faster than he is now. Keep yore hoss quiet."

They were well hidden from the highway. Guns ready, they waited while the bunch neared the wooded mound. In the van were Sidney Tynsdale in his black leather riding rig, the lean Palacio in his black hat and dark clothing, and Blackbeard Vance who had collected the outlaws composing the main company.

Hatfield watched the horsemen go by. Some wore chaps and Stetsons and had the look of being range riders. Others were city outlaws, men in plain shirts and trousers and narrow-brimmed hats. All were heavily armed with pistols, shotguns and carbines. They were strung out behind their leaders for a couple of hundred yards, and Hatfield observed the horseflesh that the majority of them rode.

Glittering eyes swept the horizon and both Vance and Tynsdale stared for a time at the little mound, but there was nothing to draw them off the route. They kept going and the dust roiled under the trotting hoofs. They disappeared over a low rise as the cotton fields began to appear.

"Now they're ahead of us," growled Ben Naler. "What next, Ranger?"

"Tynsdale ain't certain they are ahead, though he hopes we're still back in the city and he's beaten us to the run. We'll pick another route and pass 'em. Most of their hosses can't stand any kind of pace for long—yuh could see that. They'll have to go slower than we can and they'll have to rest their mounts a lot more."

Naler brightened up. "That's so. Well, come on!"

It was a matter of hard riding and a steady push. A few miles in from the highway they found a dirt road which ran through farming plantations toward the Brazos. Warming up their horses, they pushed on at a fast clip. Such swift animals could outdistance the plugs ridden by many of Tynsdale's followers in a long run.

"When yuh reckon they'll hit the Yellow Hills?" asked Naler for the hundredth time, as they pushed up a long slope toward the higher ground bounding the valley of the Colorado.

They had ridden through the long hot day and Hatfield was certain that they were ahead of Tynsdale and his bunch. He had cut back to the main highway after noon and there had been no sign of the ravening killers having passed as yet.

"I figger that Tynsdale will give his men and the hosses a breather once they get into the Yellow Hills country," answered Hatfield. "It's only fifty miles as the crow flies but the roads wind a lot and they'll stop to drink and eat and let their mounts rest. They'll have to. It will be night by the time they get over there and Vance and his gunslingers' ain't acquainted with the lay of the land, even if Tynsdale is. I think we'll have a few hours to get ready."

"I hope so," said the worn Naler fervently. "We got to save Jordan and those other folks."

Dust coated both men and horses. They had been wet to the waist after swimming the rivers and creeks on the side route, and mud had plastered them. The sun was bright and merciless.

The sun was setting behind the Yellow Hills when they passed the tiny little settlement of Stuart's Ford. There was no sign of the enemy.

"We make for Jordan's first?" inquired Naler anxiously.

"That's right."

Under the rising moon they kept on until they reached the Jordan horse farm. Lights showed in the house and Naler pressed eagerly forward.

"Watch the sentry," warned Hatfield.

Rob was on guard duty and challenged them. He was delighted to see them when they had identified themselves, and they hurried to the house. Hatfield followed Naler up on the porch. Moss Jordan jumped from his chair to greet them, but Connie ran past her father.

"Ben!"

"Connie!"

She stared up into Naler's strained features and then she was in the rancher's arms. Naler kissed her, and Moss Jordan blinked.

"Say, it looks like I'm goin' to lose my daughter," said Jordan.

Hatfield smiled. "Yuh look at it wrong, Moss. Make it yuh've won a fine young feller who will be as good as a son to yuh. He's got it all planned out for yuh. He's got as much land as you want on his ranch and he'll help yuh move out there across the Pecos so yuh'll be near 'em."

"Well, now, I don't know. I'm sort of set here."

"Please, Dad!" begged Connie softly, clinging to Naler.

"There's no time to pow-wow," said the Ranger. He quickly warned Moss Jordan of the cavalcade of death coming toward them.

Connie brought drinks for them, and hot coffee to

116

wash down a quick bite. Jordan's two men were started out to alarm the people of the hills. Others would fan out from the first places visited and carry the Ranger's word to all.

Now the tall man pinned on his badge, the silver star on silver circle, for the time to put up a fight had arrived.

He had made a tentative plan of campaign which he outlined to Jordan and Naler and they nodded in agreement.

"It's the only way," said Moss Jordan, an old soldier used to planning such affairs. "If they ever get started killin', we won't be able to check it. Ain't got enough fighters for a scrap in the open."

CHAPTER XVIII

Battle

On the stroke of midnight most of the Yellow Hills men involved had reached Jordan's and more were on the way. Sam Olliphant was there with an older son and four cowboys. Van Lewis and a brother, Mark Ellsworth, Pop Murphy, Duke Ulman and two hands, Charlie Sutton, and others came with their guns to defend themselves.

The Texas Ranger took command and told them what he intended to do. Aware of his identity now, and sufficiently impressed by his previous exhibitions of fighting power and strength of mind, they were quick to accept his leadership.

"In my opinion they'll come after Jordan first," said the Ranger. "That will fetch 'em along the south river road. I savvy just the spot where the Yellow Hills toe down almost to the water."

For what Hatfield planned they needed picks, shovels, and lanterns and Jordan could supply enough of these tools. The party rode toward Stuart's Ford to the place picked by Hatfield. A mountain spur thrust north and narrowed the valley.

"We'll dig in on that slope," said Hatfield. "Murphy, you and Ulman ride up the road a piece and stand guard. We don't aim to be surprised, though I doubt if Tynsdale comes before dawn."

His guards set, the Ranger directed the entrenching. Moss Jordan knew all about breastworks as did others who had served in the Southern armies. In order to gain protection from enemy fire, they must dig in deep enough to screen a man standing up to shoot. They made five short trench lengths along the slope over the highway, and around the bend the Ranger ordered big rocks rolled down to barricade the road. He also took his turn at digging in.

It was hard work and blistered hands, but there was no let up. Oil lanterns furnished light enough to operate by. Once when the Ranger paused to wipe sweat from his brow he curiously regarded the sides of his trench. These were dull yellow, with brownish and sometimes blackish veins streaked through.

"This is queer lookin' dirt under the topsoil, Jordan," remarked the Ranger.

Moss Jordan stepped over to stare at the uneven sides of the little trench.

"Ain't it?" he said. "But it ain't unusual, Ranger. Yuh'll find that stuff all through here. There's mountains of it. That's what gives the Yellow Hills their name."

Hatfield had been pushed hard in the fight against the ruthless, vicious Sidney Tynsdale, so during his earlier tour in the Yellow Hills he had had no hint of Tynsdale's business. Not until he had visited Houston had he discovered that Tynsdale was a manufacturer of gunpowder and allied chemicals.

Hatfield had studied mining engineering before joining the Rangers, and knew a good deal about such matters. He relinquished his shovel to a cowboy as he rolled a smoke and squatted to think it all over. Suddenly a light burst upon him.

"Now I savvy what Tynsdale's after!" he exclaimed, and set to work again, harder than ever.

When the trenches were deep enough, the Ranger screened them from the road by sticking brush and small trees into the earth in front of them. The ambush was ready.

Waiting was difficult. The armed men of the Yellow Hills rested after their labors, but there was tense anxiety in their hearts. Each man wondered if his own home and people were safe. There was a chance that Tynsdale might have come around and would strike from another direction.

Hatfield snatched forty winks. Before dawn he saddled Goldy and, leaving Moss Jordan in charge at the ambush, he rode toward Stuart's Ford.

The first gray of the new day lightened the sky when he sighted the enemy. With Tynsdale, Vance and Felipe Palacio in the van, the killers were coming!

The Ranger pushed the golden sorrel around the curve and pulled up in full sight of his foes.

Tynsdale saw him first. The chief shouted hoarsely and raised an arm to point out the tall rider who had fought so hard against Tynsdale's overwhelming power. Vance and Palacio and others in the sordid crew also recognized Hatfield.

The new light touched the silver star within the silver circle. Tynsdale knew then that he was a Texas Ranger and for that reason the powder manufacturer had to kill him. Tynsdale dared not leave such an enemy alive to balk his plans.

Hatfield feigned surprise at sight of the great band of killers. He uttered a Rebel yell and whipped up a Colt to fire at them. A man clapped a hand to his arm and Vance and his men surged forward, shooting as they came.

The sorrel took Hatfield out ahead, out of easy pistol range. They were baying like fierce dogs on a blood trail and the speed picked up until they were strung out and rushing along at full tilt. Hatfield did not want them to miss the ambush, so meant to lead them to it.

The faster they came, led on by the Ranger, the better for Moss Jordan and his hidden forces. As Hatfield had believed they must, Tynsdale's party had stopped to rest themselves and their mounts, to eat and drink before starting their attack on Jordan's. They had gone on the old theory that the first touch of dawn was always the best time to strike, before people were up, and yet with enough light to see details.

Such a force as Tynsdale had brought along could easily overwhelm single victims. A determined rush on a house would carry the howling, killing gunslingers through to the building, and the thin defense any one family could offer would mean little.

Sidney Tynsdale, in his leather outfit and Stetson, had his reversed bandanna bunched at his bearded chin. The manufacturer dropped back in the eager crush of riders pushing on the Ranger's trail. Palacio stayed close to his master. Blackbeard Vance whooped it up savagely, egging on his men.

The morning light was up when they swerved on the road to skirt the hulking mountain spur hemming in the valley. On the right toward the river was a rocky slope, uneven for fast riding.

Hatfield glanced up. Jordan had his riflemen hidden in the screened trenches. The toe of the hill cut off the barricade from the direction in which the enemy were coming. The Ranger made the turn, leaped from his saddle and scampered up the sliding bank toward his friends.

"Go on, run off, Goldy!" he cried.

The trained sorrel swerved, picking his way down the hill toward the brush screen where the river bank dropped to the stream. He moved fast and bullets sent after him missed him. Soon the gelding was safe among the trees.

The howling, angry gunhands, however, were intent on the man rather than his horse. They came around the turn at full speed as the Ranger, panting for breath, jumped into a trench and shouted:

"Open up, boys! Let 'em have it."

Jordan's men fired. It was a deadly, withering volley cutting the enemy flank. Vance's killers turned in their leather seats. All they could do was to send ineffectual pistol shots back at the screened trenches. But only bobbing Stetsons and faces showed at which to aim.

Behind the first riders the main gang piled up, horses rearing, and shrieking in alarm, jogging against the mounts in front. Blackbeard Vance was bellowing frantic commands as he tried to break up the growing melee. Confused by the sudden, smashing blow, the bunch from Houston looked for escape.

Lead plugged into mustang ribs and into human flesh, cutting Vance's fighters. Some sought to get away by speed, but the barricade of boulders ahead blocked the road. They swerved down the uneven slope and pelted toward the river. But horses went down on the treacherous stretch and then half a dozen marksmen, posted at the drop of the river bank, opened fire.

Churning in the narrow space, the gunslingers sought to turn and ride back the way they had come.

"Ambush! Ambush!" screamed a high-pitched voice over and over.

Men fell in the crush, cut by the flying hoofs of their own horses. Vance's efforts to rally them and regain fighting order were lost in the shuffle. With such fellows, when so pressed, it became every man for himself. They were in it for profit, money and possible loot. Determined resistance and a loss of the odds would break such a force.

The Houston men were beginning to slug and shoot at

one another as they found themselves blocked in the surging mess. Blind fury possessed them, as they sought to run away and could not because their companions were in the way.

A few lucky ones managed to skirt between the barricade and the river and by spurring their mustangs in a mad dash, reached the road beyond. But these made no attempt to help their trapped comrades. They galloped on as fast as they could go, hunting for escape. Others at the extreme rear were able to swing and retreat.

Around Blackbeard Vance rallied a few more determined rascals. Vance was shooting back at the heads he saw. His beard bristled and his eyes flamed with red hate.

"They'll give up if Vance falls!" thought the Ranger.

He was down the line but he rose up and took careful aim, aware that Vance saw him and was turning his gun on the tall officer. The silver star within the circle glinted in the morning light as Hatfield's thumb rose from the hammer and the big pistol spoke.

Flame flashed from Vance's gun and Hatfield heard the bullet whiz past his ear. Vance threw up his arms and stood up high in his saddle. His eyes seemed as wide as saucers for an instant, then he collapsed. The dancing stallion under him threw off the heavy body as Vance's legs relaxed their grip. The killer slid to the road. Mustangs immediately closed about him and Vance was no longer in sight.

Wild slugs missed the Ranger as he ducked down, and then came up again to peek over the trench bulge. The opposition was dying. It was only spasmodic now with no direction. The big Ranger jumped out of the trench and ran along the steep slope.

"Surrender!" he bawled, his stentorian voice ringing over the clang of the battle. "Surrender in the name of Texas! Throw down, outlaws!"

The quailing gunslingers saw Jim Hatfield in all his magnificent fighting trim. They were already beaten by the Ranger strategy and tactics. Many threw in their guns and raised their hands high so they would not be killed by the marksmen inside the trenches.

As the stronger found themselves deserted by their comrades they, too, lost heart. Colts and carbines were dropped and hands raised. The Houston outlaws begged for mercy, pleading for life. It was better to chance a prison sentence than to die under those biting rifles.

The fight ended quickly as the killers surrendered.

"Come on, tie 'em up," Jim Hatfield called. "There's plenty of prisoners for yuh, gents."

Moss Jordan and the men of the Yellow Hills came swarming out of the trenches. The high-pitched Rebel yell rang out as they slid down to the road, and while some covered the captives, others secured their hands and pulled them off their horses. They were lined up against the wall of the bluff and held by menacing, scowling marksmen.

But Sidney Tynsdale was not among the sullen company they had roped in. Blackbeard Vance was dead, shot by a Ranger bullet and crushed under the sharp hoofs of his own horses.

"I'll have to get Tynsdale or it's no go," muttered the Ranger.

He was weary and cut up by the hard scrap. He had lost sight of Tynsdale in the heat of the fight and the manufacturer had been hidden from him by the bulging spur.

"Tynsdale must have been able to turn and ride back," Hatfield said to Moss Jordan. "He's the real cause of yore troubles. If we let him go he'll be back with a worse bunch."

Palacio, too, was gone. The dark skinned Spaniard was never far from Tynsdale and they had stayed well to the rear when the shooting and pursuit of the Ranger had begun. The crafty Tynsdale had got away.

The tall officer whistled up the golden sorrel. Goldy

came up the slope, climbing toward the road. Ben Naler, who had fought bravely through the battle, was helping Moss Jordan, for the Yellow Hills contingent was small to guard the large number of prisoners. The desperadoes would be watching for a chance to bolt, when they regained their breath and nerve.

"I'll go after Tynsdale myself," decided Hatfield.

Mounting the golden sorrel he started on Sidney Tynsdale's trail.

CHAPTER XIX

Paid Up

Sidney Tynsdale must pay for what he had done! That thought was in the Ranger's mind as he rode at a fast clip on his mission. It was still with him when he entered the little settlement of Stuart's Ford. He did not mean for Tynsdale to get back to Houston where the manufacturer had many friends and cronies, a battery of expensive lawyers to shield him from the law.

In a glance the tall officer could sweep the main street of the town. In the bright morning sunshine Stuart's Ford was as lively as it ever was, with a few housewives out marketing and children playing in the meadows. Dogs, pigs and chickens were in the back yards. The constable was dozing in front of the little lockup down the plaza. Several saddle horses and a couple of teams stood at the racks.

The grim stranger, marked by battle and the hard chase he had made, rode straight down the center of the road, glancing right and left. The gray-green eyes had a dark coldness in them now and his loaded Colts rode ready at his hips. The golden sorrel stepped high with the pride of his calling.

In front of the livery stable stood two lathered, spur-gouged mustangs with blood running down their flanks. They were heaving, and had been run almost to death. A wrangler was taking the saddle off one and transferring it to the back of a fresh black, while a chestnut gelding already wore the second hull which had been cinched tight.

Sidney Tynsdale emerged from the Palace bar and at once he saw the big officer coming. Tynsdale gave a sharp cry. He whipped a pistol from his holster and fired twice. One bullet came within a foot of the moving Ranger's ear.

Tynsdale jumped back as Hatfield pulled a Colt and took aim. Hatfield shifted his hand and the big revolver boomed. Tynsdale leaped, turned, and Palacio ran from the saloon and threw himself between his master and the Ranger as Hatfield let go once more. Palacio had a gun up and was taking careful aim.

Palacio caught the Ranger's bullet and folded up in the middle. As he went down, Tynsdale made the door of the bar and disappeared inside.

Hatfield jumped to the road and ran toward the Palace, gun in hand. He ducked under the rail and went up on the low veranda of the saloon. He paused, seeing Tynsdale running for the back.

"Halt, Tynsdale!" he shouted. His stentorian voice echoed in the empty barroom.

Tynsdale glanced back. He had his gun out and in desperation he raised it and fired. The slug cut a long splinter from the frame of the front door and the Ranger was slashed by a flying sliver of wood. A woman screamed in the hotel annex and the proprietor, who had been cleaning up, ducked behind the bar.

Hatfield rushed in. "Surrender!" he shouted, giving Tynsdale another chance to submit to arrest.

Tynsdale had almost reached the back way out. His eyes glinted with his hate of the Ranger who had run him to earth. The blunt manufacturer turned and slid to a halt. He was crouched, and his teeth were bared in a snarl.

Hatfield kept coming at him.

"*Mort!* Death to the Rangers!" shrieked Tynsdale.

He had a close target and the big Ranger came steadily on. Tynsdale threw up his pistol. Blood suffused his bearded cheeks. His eyes were as round as saucers as he fired.

The Ranger moved with the speed of trained precision. Seeing that Tynsdale meant to kill, would not give in, Hatfield shot a breath ahead of his enemy.

He heard the near miss of his foe's bullet. But Tynsdale was already staggering. Blood showed on the spade beard and Tynsdale dropped his revolver and raised a small, jeweled hand to his throat. Then he half-turned and fell in the sawdust. . . .

Late that afternoon, Jim Hatfield addressed the men of the Yellow Hills as they gathered at Moss Jordan's farm to talk over the battle. Connie had served food and drink and the pretty girl stood with Ben Naler's protective arm around her as they listened to the Ranger.

"Yuh have all wondered what it was that caused Sidney Tynsdale to strike yuh," Hatfield said. "It was Tynsdale who sicked Dowie Burke on yuh and gave Burke that list of death with yore names on it. Burke was to kill all on that list. Yuh owned the Yellow Hills and Tynsdale wanted the land. He knew he could pick up the properties for a song, if not for nothin', by destroyin' the owners.

"I didn't find out till last night what Tynsdale wanted. When I located him in Houston I learned he was a gunpowder manufacturer. He owned a big business there and was makin' plenty of money, but aimed to expand. Gunpowder's composed of saltpetre, which is potassium nitrate, of charcoal, and of sulphur.

"The sulphur is hard to get right now and Tynsdale figgered on makin' hisself sort of a sulphur king. These Yellow Hills are actually mountains of sulphur, and that's what Tynsdale wanted.

"He learned of it and checked up, found it was so. He kept it quiet and tried to take yore homes. There was a big fortune and world power in it for Tynsdale and he wasn't the sort who would worry over gettin' rid of a few folks."

A murmur rose from the company.

"This here sulphur is worth big money?" asked Moss Jordan.

"Yes, suh," declared the Ranger. "It's used not only for gunpowder but in makin' matches, fireworks, medicines and bleachin' compounds. I've talked with most of yuh, as yuh savvy, and from what yuh say the deposits underlie the entire Yellow Hills. There must be enough to supply the whole United States, mebbe the world. Mountains of it, I tell yuh."

"We're rich, then!" cried Duke Ulman, usually silent, but awakened to speech by the Ranger's information.

"That's right," Hatfield nodded. "Yuh can sell out for plenty." He circled to Moss Jordan. "Jordan, they'll be diggin' here steady for years, I figger," he said. "Air will be full of sulphur dust and all. It ain't goin' to be a good place to raise horses."

"No, it ain't," agreed Jordan.

Connie and Naler were watching closely.

"I know a mighty good place yuh could move to," Hatfield drawled on. "Across the Pecos, where Ben Naler has a ranch. He'll give yuh as much land as yuh can use."

"I shore will, Mr. Jordan!" cried Naler.

"Please, Dad!" begged Connie.

Moss Jordan's face was wreathed in smiles. "Of course. I aimed to anyways. I'll go."

"This is as good a time as any to tell yore neighbors that Connie's marryin' Ben Naler, ain't it?" asked the Ranger softly.

The girl flushed rosily as Naler held her hand and Moss Jordan blessed them.

In Austin headquarters Captain Bill McDowell heard the Ranger's report on the trouble in the Yellow Hills.

"Yuh don't look like Cupid much," said McDowell critically. "Still yuh brought off the trick. Yuh're rugged, and that's what it took to settle Tynsdale's hash. Good work, Ranger."

Hatfield took quiet satisfaction in McDowell's approbation. The old captain did not say too much but he said enough to indicate his high opinion of the tall officer.

There was always new business at Ranger headquarters. Complaints flowed in from every point of the compass, from the thorn jungles of the southeast, from the sultry Gulf Coast, from the forests along the Red River, from the fabulous Panhandle and the Trans-Pecos, the Rio Grande and the tremendous heartland.

Always there were new rascals bobbing up to challenge the law, too tough for local authorities to handle or based where there was no sheriff. Then the Rangers must ride.

McDowell rattled a sheaf of reports. It was a new problem and as usual with the hard ones he had to deal with it meant danger of death to the investigating officer. Hatfield listened to the new complaint. Outlaws were operating along the Red River and good men were being shot up and put upon.

Happiest when on the trail, Jim Hatfield made ready. Soon the old captain stood in the sunshine outside his office, again, waving farewell to his star operative as the Ranger on the golden sorrel moved off to carry the law to the Lone Star empire.